Blackmailed by the Billionaire

Elizabeth Lennox

CONTENTS

Chapter 1

Information. It was arguably more powerful than money, Nikolai thought as he put the report down on the desk, his fingers forming a pyramid as he considered the data he had just received.

A sense of triumph filled Nikolai. His midnight blue eyes looked away from the words on the report he'd just been given and out to the stunning view of the sun rising over the buildings of London, enjoying the feeling of triumph as it washed over him like a satin touch.

Patience had always been his best asset, he thought. And now, revenge would be sweet.

Tabitha MacComber would beg for mercy. The only question was whether Nik would allow it. His mind remembered her smiling green eyes, her flawless, porcelain skin and a body any man would happily die to possess. Of course, hidden behind that stunningly beautiful façade was a cunning and mercenary nature that had blindsided him four years ago.

Nikolai Andretti smiled coldly as he looked back down at the stock prices on his computer. It was not a smile of amusement although it was filled with deep satisfaction. His eyes quickly scanned down the list of stock prices. When he found the line he was looking for, he raised one eyebrow and mentally did some calculations. He had waited patiently for this situation to come about and now that victory was almost his, he wanted to savor the feeling, let it slide down like a woman's tender caress. It had actually taken less time than he'd anticipated but the keenness of victory was no less satisfying for the speed with which her downfall had come.

Setting the delicate china cup filled with fragrant coffee down on the white linen table cloth, he reflected on how the world seemed to right itself, provide opportunities. With a deep sense of amusement and irony, he leaned back in the leather chair and considered his options. Because of the mess she was currently in, there were several possibilities open to him, and all would end in the same way. He just had to choose the most effective. He would have to conduct the transactions discreetly, he knew. No one could know about the stock purchases until he was ready to reveal his hand.

Quickly analyzing the options and calculating the costs as well as the risks associated with each scenario, he made a decision. Raising the phone, he gave curt instructions to his personal assistant, then ended the call abruptly, knowing his assistant would be able to fill in the blanks accurately. Standing up, he looked out one of the floor to ceiling windows that made up three walls of his office. Being on the top floor of this particular skyscraper, he had an extraordinary view of London. Today though, he saw nothing of the striking horizon as the sun rose over the vast city. His mind's eye was remembering the perfect beauty of Tabitha MacComber, her startling blue eyes, her tiny waist that flared gently out to slender hips, ending in long legs that a man could fantasize about forever.

The lying, deceitful bitch that still occasionally haunted his dreams would finally be exorcised from his mind. He wanted her. After seeing her smiling face in the report, he had to accept that reality. Tabitha MacComber was incredibly lovely but also the only woman who had tricked him so completely, gotten under his skin and then made a fool of him. Nikolai considered himself extremely experienced when it came to women specifically and people in general. He knew most of their tricks and thought they were amusing at times. But Tabitha had duped him. Her air of sweetness and fragility, innocence, had definitely deceived him.

But now it was his turn to hold the reins. He would have her, on his terms, on his turf, for as long as he wanted her. And there would be nothing she could do to stop him this time.

Chapter 2

"Good morning, Nancy," Tabitha MacComber said, smiling brightly at the woman sitting just outside the executive board room. Tabitha instantly noted the worried look in the other woman's soft, brown eyes. "Are you feeling okay?" she asked with curiosity. Nancy had been the receptionist at MacComber Industries for longer than Tabitha was alive and she was always cheerful and ready with a smile.

Nancy nodded, but the anxiety stayed in her eyes. "I'm fine, Ms. MacComber."

Tabitha could see that the woman was nervous but had no idea why. She made a mental note to stop by and talk with her, find out if there was something genuinely wrong. Maybe there were problems with her daughter's first pregnancy.

At the moment, Tabitha was running a few minutes late so she pushed through the double oak doors that had stood guard outside the board room of MacComber Industries for the last hundred years.

The silence that greeted her as she breezed through the door almost made her steps falter, but she continued down the long room to the opposite end of the table, pasting a bright smile onto her face. "Gentlemen," she said to the fourteen grim-looking men who were already seated at the polished oak conference table. The fact that they were all seated at the appointed meeting time was unprecedented. "What an extraordinary event to be starting on time!" she joked. When she received no response, she quickly placed her pink purse under the table and opened the leather notebook expectantly.

"Is something wrong?" she asked, looking at all the faces. "I can't imagine why everyone is so tense," she started to say and tucked a blond curl back behind her ear. "After all, the stock price is finally creeping back up. That's good news as far as I can tell," she said, smiling cheerfully at the rest of the table. Again, no response. Only forbidding faces looking down at their notebooks.

"Charlie," she said, turning to grin gaily at a man mid-way down the table. "Why are you looking so glum? You should be celebrating. Didn't your son just marry Melody Miller down in Australia? You should be thrilled. What a match!" she said, hiding her abhorrence for society marriages. She knew these men lived and died for them. She shivered in revulsion but pushed the memory of her own failed marriage aside.

When she only received a tense smile from Charlie, she turned to another man who was sitting closer. "Mark, didn't you just receive news of grandchild number five? That's wonderful to hear!" she enthused.

Mark nodded and she received a brief glimpse of a smile, but it quickly faded.

The tension was odd and she wished she could figure out what had happened to cause such behavior in men who generally joked and laughed about numerous issues before finally getting down to business.

"Okay, I give up," she laughed. "Does someone want to enlighten me as to why it seems that the sky is falling?"

Nelson Miller cleared his throat and sat forward. Nelson was the current chief operating officer of MacComber Industries and a sweet, if somewhat hesitant, man in his early forties. She noticed him glance behind her momentarily and hesitate but she focused all of her attention on the man, knowing that there was only a landscape painting on the wall behind her.

"It's like this, Tabitha," he started, his fingers nervously swiping at the lock of hair that had fallen free of its usually perfect setting. "You remember how we invested in that factory in Dorset?" he started off.

"Of course," she smiled. "Are you telling me that I was wrong? That the factory has actually started to show a profit? Because if that's true, I think I owe you a very large apology," she said, smiling encouragingly at him. "I didn't think that plan would work and it was a large amount of money to throw at a risky scheme."

Nelson leaned forward, his face turning red all of a sudden. "Now see here," he started off, huffing slightly in his anger, "it would have worked. There were just some complications." He glanced behind her again, then down at his paper. "The distribution venues just weren't adequate for our needs," he explained. "And there was poor management that we weren't aware of."

Tabitha smothered a spark of anger. "I thought you said that you'd met with the management of the factory and they were quite adequate," she countered, maintaining her smile despite her frustrations with the man's continued incompetence.

"Well, the deal was about to close and I didn't…." he trailed off, leaving the sentence unfinished.

Tabitha's eyes sharpened and she had to struggle to not show her irritation at the man. "You mean you didn't even speak to the management of the factory? Nelson, do you think that was wise? I even offered to go out there and talk with them before the purchase deadline."

Nelson stood up and banged his fist on the table. "You are a woman," he yelled angrily. "You couldn't possibly have the skills necessary to judge a man's character and tell if he is an adequate manager."

Tabitha bowed her head, realizing that their sexist attitudes were welling up. Some of the other men were actually nodding, their frowns deepening and she had to grit her teeth. "Well, then. From what I'm gathering as I read between the lines, the purchase of that particular factory was a mistake. Am I correct?" she asked, looking around the table at the gentlemen. Many of them looked away. Some pushed their pens or papers around. But none of them acknowledged her question.

"I think I was the one that was cautioning against this purchase," she said evenly, shuddering at the cost of the factory and wondering what kind of financial impact this setback would have on the company. "Okay. We made a mistake," she said, including herself in that decision. She hadn't argued loudly enough against the issue so she was part of the problem. "What do we have to do to clean it up?" she asked to the group of men.

When none of them answered, she glanced to the other side of the table. "George, what do you think? How soon can we sell off the factory and recoup our losses?" she asked.

Nelson shook his head. "You're out of your league, Tabitha. Why don't you run off and go shopping and let us handle this situation?" he said, his tone patronizing. "I'll even take you out for dinner once the dust has settled."

Tabitha gripped her pen until her knuckles were white, struggling to hold her temper.

She ignored his offer of dinner and continued, "Well, it looks like we're all in a bit of a pickle, wouldn't you say? And I doubt sending me on a shopping trip is going to solve that problem. Do any of you?" she asked, looking at each of the elderly men, disheartened to know now what they actually thought about her.

The chuckle behind her was terrifying in its familiarity and an electric shock immediately went through her body at the sound.

Was that…..no. Impossible, she told herself, frozen in the big, leather chair. He wouldn't be here….there's no way….!

It just couldn't be, she told herself. Her breath caught in her throat and her blood seemed to freeze in her veins as her mind recognized the voice behind that laughter. Even her body understood who was behind her although her mind still refused to believe what every cell was telling her. It simply couldn't be him. She turned bit by bit, the world moving in slow motion as she swiveled in her leather chair to face the owner of the deep voice. Praying that it wasn't so, her eyes widening as she took in the man leaning casually against the wall.

"You!" she spat out, her whole mind instantly forgetting about the fourteen men seated around the table as her world focused on the one man that had been behind her for the past fifteen minutes.

Nikolai Andretti!

"What are you doing here!" she demanded, standing up in an effort to gain some height and lose some of the fear that was quickly spreading throughout her body, freezing her mind. How could this man make her instantly feel something so strong? It had been four years! Couldn't the impact of his presence dim somewhat?

He didn't rise to her angry challenge, one eyebrow rising slightly the only indication that he had heard her question. He didn't even bother to stand up, but continued to lean casually against the wall, appearing as if this whole mess was highly amusing to him. "Good morning, Tabitha. I see the heart grows fonder with time, does it not?" he asked sardonically.

Tabitha's whole body started shaking as she took in the presence of the man that could evoke so many memories, so many painful, dreadful and yet also beautiful memories for her. She pushed those thoughts and feelings aside and squared her shoulders. "I'm not sure who invited you here but it is completely inappropriate. This is a board meeting and only board members and large stock holders are permitted," she stated slowly, afraid that her voice might fail if she didn't concentrate on each syllable.

Her stomach muscles tightened as his sensuous mouth eased into a triumphant smile. His midnight blue eyes darkened to black. "Ah, *pethia meu*," he said, pushing away from the wall and walking toward her. He was so tall, Tabitha had to push her head back in order to continue to hold his gaze. "As you so aptly put it a few moments ago, the stock price has gone up considerably. Have you not stopped to consider how that occurred?"

Tabitha opened her mouth, her mind frantically working to come up with a plausible explanation. "I assumed it was the factory coming on line."

His smile was lethal, giving her ample clues that her assumption was incorrect. "And now that you know that the factory has not come on line as expected, is in fact pulling your company into bankruptcy, what would be your next guess?"

Tabitha thought hard, wishing she could come up with some other reason. Frantically working through all the scenarios, she came to the final, and worst, possibility. Her eyes snapping to his in disbelief and horror. "No!" she whispered.

Nikolai smiled again, his sexy mouth curving in triumphant pleasure. "I see you've finally come to the correct conclusion," he said with a great deal of gratification.

"That's impossible!" she countered. "All of these men own stock and, combined, they have a controlling interest. There's no way you could be a stock holder with any kind of power in this company."

Nik looked around at the men, none of whom were willing to hold his gaze. "I'm afraid you have put your trust into the wrong source," he said softly. "Again." He let those words float in the air for a long moment before continuing. "Each of these men were more than willing to sell their stock in your precious company. I now own fifty-five percent of the stock. It is mine to do with as I please," he said, his eyes hard and brilliant with the success of his acquisition.

Tabitha pulled back, her hatred for this man and all he knew about her was too painful to endure. "Why on earth would you bother with a company so small?" she demanded. "You're reputation is that you take over billion dollar companies. What is the appeal of MacComber Industries? Don't you have bigger fish to mercilessly gobble up?" she demanded. "Our revenue is only in the millions. We employ less than five hundred people. I would have thought we were beneath your notice," she said, knowing that he could buy and sell MacComber Industries a hundred times over and never even blink at the impact to his personal bank balance.

He shrugged his shoulders slightly. "When an opportunity arrives, I jump at it," he said coolly.

It was hard for her to believe anyone could be so casual about an amount of money that, to her, was enormous. But she knew that, to him, it was almost insignificant. "An opportunity for what?" she asked breathlessly. "This is nothing but petty vindictiveness and I'm not going to let you get away with it."

Nikolai surveyed her flushed, angry expression without any outward reaction. "Perhaps this is a conversation we should have in private," he said softly.

"Don't bother with niceties," she replied. "I have nothing to say to you." She crossed her arms over her chest, her chin going up a notch in challenge.

Without another word, he looked down the board room table at the men behind her. Instantly, fourteen elderly men stood up and hurried out of the room. Within thirty seconds, all of them had disappeared, closing the door softly and leaving Tabitha alone with the one man in the world she hated.

"What were you saying?" he asked once they were alone.

Her arms dropped in defeat and she couldn't look up at him. "You have a photographic memory," she snapped, turning her back on him in a defensive gesture. "You remember exactly what the accusation was," she said and took several steps away, afraid to let him see her expression.

Nikolai smiled and nodded. "Yes. In fact, you are right," he said, his Greek accent coming through as his amusement surfaced. "Revenge," he said simply.

She spun back around to face him, her eyes searching his dark, mysterious eyes in the hopes that he was joking. The blood actually chilled in her veins when she realized that he wasn't. Her worst fears had come true. Nikolai being here was bad enough. But that he wanted revenge that was awful. Terrifying!

"And what if I told you that revenge has already been had?" she asked, the fear coming through to her voice in the form of a slight break despite her efforts to appear calm and in control of this horrifying situation.

Nikolai shook his head. "Ah, my dear Tabitha. I don't think you know the meaning of the word," he said, one hand coming up to run a finger down the soft, creamy texture of her skin. "But I intend to remedy that," he explained.

She pulled her face away, desperate to end the touch that, even after so many years, could still heat her body. She was ashamed of her reaction and couldn't hide the anger from him. "No!"

He pulled back abruptly and dropped his hand. "In fact, yes." He moved away and poured her a glass of icy water from a side table, handing her the glass.

Tabitha took it with shaking fingers, unaware of how he could have read her mind so accurately. Drinking the water quickly, she placed the empty glass behind her on the oak table. "What are you telling me?"

His smile broadened. "I'm telling you that we have some unfinished business. I intend to close out that brief period in our lives. But this time, we will have a more satisfying end. And we will do it on my terms," he said.

She shivered, the memories of how they had parted coming back to her conscious mind.

He chuckled. "I can see that you are thinking about the same memory as I am."

"No," she said, rubbing her forehead in frustration and an overwhelming need to find a place to hide, perhaps start the day over again with a less horrifying beginning. "I don't know what you are talking about."

His eyes sharpened, reminding her of painful shards of glass. "Then let me enlighten you," he started and moved closer so there was barely an inch of space between their bodies. "That last night we shared together, you were all hot and heavy for me, willing to do anything, just as into the moment as I was. Then you stopped, claiming modesty and virtue, something we both know you have neither of!" he said calmly, but with venom in his eyes. "Since you decided to go off and marry someone else, I was left hanging."

"I won't believe you were alone for long!" she spat at him, the pain of her last phone call to him hitting her with painful clarity. "If in fact, you were ever waiting on me to come to your bed?" she asked, stepping back so she could breathe. "I'm guessing there were many women already clamoring for your pathetic brand of romance." She walked away from the table, needing space away from his body so she could focus.

Nikolai followed her, not giving her any room to think, cornering her against the wall. His dark eyes revealed nothing as he said, "Ah, no, my sweet Tabitha. There is no retreat for you. Let me explain exactly what is going to happen. We're going to make love, you and I. Over and over again.

Until I have had my fill of you. And this time, there will be no teasing," he said harshly. "I will have you whenever and however I want."

Her body reacted strongly but not in the way she wished. Her mind was remembering the exquisitely beautiful kisses they had shared four years ago and her body ached to experience that kind of magic again.

Shaking her head to rid herself of those ridiculous fantasies, she turned away from him, not wanting to look at the man who had destroyed her dreams all those years ago. "That's not possible," she said, her voice low and pained.

His smile was a combination of triumph and male arrogance as he said, "It will still be your choice."

"Then my choice is no. Adamantly no!" she shot back at him.

He chuckled at her vehemence. "Perhaps you should hear the terms before making your decision."

"There's nothing you can say that will convince me to sleep with you," she said angrily.

He reached up and touched her shoulder length, brown, curly hair, capturing a lock between his fingers and rubbing the silken strands, testing their softness. "Since sleeping will be the last thing on my mind when we get to my bed, I will agree with you on that point," he said evenly.

"You're disgusting!" she said and pulled her hair out of his fingers. "Leave me alone!"

He pulled back and walked away, straightening the cuffs on his snowy white shirt. "Very well. I'll start the sales proceedings immediately."

Those words chilled her to the bone. "Wh…What are you talking about?" she asked, straightening now that he wasn't standing over her, trying to intimidate her.

His eyes were cold and hard as he looked across the expanse of the conference room at her. "I'll sell off every piece of this company, starting with the headquarters. All of these people will be out of a job by the end of this month." He flicked a glance across the room and started walking toward the doors.

Tabitha didn't think that things could get worse, but his words proved her wrong. "Are you kidding?" she asked, moving quickly to stand in front of him, blocking the double door exit.

His smile was merciless. "Have I ever joked about anything? Especially something this serious?"

Tabitha shook her head slowly. "No," she finally said through a painfully tight throat.

"I can assure you that I have not started at this juncture in my life. Business is business," he said simply, shrugging his shoulders.

"You're reducing sex down to a business arrangement? And you'll put over five hundred people out of work simply because I won't sleep with you?" Her shock was making her mind work slowly. She just couldn't fathom anyone acting in such a heartless manner.

"Absolutely," he said without remorse. "I've found that most liaisons are basically a business arrangement. Women always want something; a trinket, a vacation, or their picture in the paper connecting their name to mine." His voice softened slightly when he added, "But I can also guarantee that none of them leave my bed unsatisfied. I take great pleasure in ensuring each of my companions leave with a smile."

"Stop it," she said, covering her ears with her hands. "I don't want to hear these things! Leave all those other women out of this conversation. If you hate me so much, why in the world would you do this to me? Why would you spend millions of dollars buying controlling stock in this company?"

His eyes traveled down her body and she was ashamed when her nipples peaked under his knowing look. She hated that her body reacted, willing her trembling anticipation to go away. "There are some things the mind ignores when it comes to pleasures of the flesh. I saw your picture in the paper last month and realized that I still wanted you. Therefore, I have found a way to have you. It's all in your hands."

His dark blue eyes glittered moments before he said, "Example in point," and without any further warning, his strong, muscular arms pulled her against his body, one arm wrapping around her waist while his other hand came up to tangle in her curls, bringing her head up only a moment before his mouth covered hers. He took advantage of her gasp, his tongue moving into her mouth and mating with hers.

Tabitha was stunned and her mind stopped working as her body took over. She reacted without thought to his kiss, her body glorying in the amazing feel of his hands, his lips and his tongue as he showed her again how wonderful and skilled he was as a lover. She was unaware of the soft moans that escaped her as his mouth caressed hers, his hard body molding against her softer one.

He pulled free suddenly and looked down at her for a long moment, noting with satisfaction the stunned expression in her soft, blue eyes. "You have twenty-four hours to contact me. If I don't hear from you, the auction begins tomorrow at noon," he said and flipped a business card from a pocket, handing it to her. A moment later, he was gone, leaving Tabitha staring at the expensive velum business card, her whole body trembling in reaction to both his kiss and his ultimatum.

Chapter 3

That evening, sitting in the big house her father had left to her, she cooked her lonely dinner but couldn't swallow any of it. The tears she'd been holding at bay all day slowly fell, eventually tapering off as she stared out at the night blackened window. She didn't see anything though. Her mind was moving back to that fateful meeting when she'd first met Nik. He'd been so different then. So....amazing.

She'd been standing at the train station waiting for her father to pick her up. She had only just returned home from finishing school and was looking forward to a relaxing summer before she started to look for some sort of employment. She hoped her father would allow her to work in the family company, but knew he was pretty old fashioned and didn't think women should work. Marriage was probably what he was hoping for, but she was confident enough that she could convince him otherwise.

She heard the motorcycle before she could see it. The flashy red zoomed around the curve, then came to a quick halt as the rider looked around. When his eyes lit on her, the helmet lifted and dark, penetrating eyes looked her up and down. "Good afternoon," his deep voice said.

Tabitha looked around nervously. The train station was on the outskirts of town, surrounded on three sides with trees. It was relatively isolated, but she saw several pedestrians walking along a side street which assured her that she wasn't completely alone.

"Good afternoon," she replied nervously, smiling politely even though the man's tight denims and leather jacket showed her that he was absolutely gorgeous.

"Would you be able to tell me how to get to Burnham Street?" he asked, pulling a map out of a small glove compartment of his motorcycle.

Having lived in this small town all her life, Tabitha was very aware of how the streets intersected and changed names several times. If one didn't know the streets, it was easy to become turned around.

"Of course," she said, stepping forward to the edge of the platform and raised her arm to point over at the right. "If you go down that street, then turn left again, you'll be on Burnham Street." She paused before continuing, "Why do you want Burnham Street?" she asked, knowing it was in one of the shadier sections of the town. Despite his motorcycle and jeans, he still didn't seem like the type to be frequenting the harsher side of her fair city.

The man's sexy smile made her stomach flip flop and her heart beat accelerate. "I have a meeting with someone at one," he explained. "Do you need a lift?" he asked.

Tabitha blushed for some reason but shook her head. "No, thank you. My father will be along soon to pick me up. But thank you for the offer. I don't want to make you late for your meeting." She folded her hands primly in front of her, wondering why her mind was drifting to thoughts of this daring, dangerous man without that leather jacket.

The audacious man winked at her, then put his helmet back on. Revving the engine to his motorcycle, he waved back to her before speeding off in the direction she'd given him. Tabitha smiled, her mind instantly forming a romantic scene where he carried her off on his motorcycle to his country cabin and the two of them fell madly in love. She shook her head, pushing the silly fantasy aside, then picked up her book and sat down on the bench to wait for her father. It was a lovely spring afternoon and she didn't mind sitting out in the sun for the few minutes while she waited, sure that her father would be along any moment.

Next thing she knew, the motor cycle was buzzing right back up the street. Tabitha looked at her watch and gasped. Over an hour had passed but she'd been so absorbed in her mystery book that she hadn't even noticed that her father had obviously forgotten about her.

"Hello again," the man said, pulling up alongside the train station platform and setting up the kick stand before taking off his helmet again. "Looks like your ride didn't come along. How about if we put your luggage in a storage locker and I get you a cup of coffee?" By the time he finished his suggestion, he was already standing up on the platform, his long legs carrying him quickly so he was standing in front of her as he stared down into her embarrassed face.

"I think you're quite right," she said, looking down the road again as if her father's car would suddenly appear. "I guess he must have forgotten."

"He?" the man asked.

Tabitha flushed, realizing the unspoken question. "My father."

"Ah. Good," he replied. "You can't stay here on the train platform indefinitely. It doesn't look like you have a cell phone and it's getting late. I'm sure this is a very nice town but it probably isn't safe for you out here alone." He leaned down slightly and said in a teasing, conspiratorial tone, "I promise I'm a very trustworthy fellow. So how about that coffee?"

Tabitha looked down at her skirt, then back up at his gorgeous face. "I don't think I'm appropriately dressed to ride with you," she said, the disappointment written on her face.

He leaned forward again and winked at her. "I promise not to look if you pull your skirt up," he said, reading her mind.

Tabitha could only laugh at his wit but she was thrilled someone as handsome as he was willing to pass the time of day with her. "Deal," she replied, feeling daring and naughty but extremely pretty with his sexy eyes daring her to come with him. Normally only the very upright, preppy boys chatted with her and this man was refreshingly….sexy!

He didn't reply, simply smiled again and picked up her heavy suitcases effortlessly, storing them in one of the large lockers, locking it and handing her the key.

True to his word, he got onto the motorcycle and stared straight ahead while she climbed onto the back, handing her the only helmet. "By the way, my name's Nikolai," he said, turning his head slightly so the sound traveled her way.

"I'm Tabitha," she replied.

Tabitha timidly put her hands on his shoulders as he started the engine. "You're going to have to hold on a lot tighter than that if you don't want to fall off the back," he warned only moments before accelerating rapidly. Tabitha grabbed his waist and locked her legs around his hips, terrified of the alternative. She didn't mind hugging this man though, a dangerous thrill going through her as he moved through the village streets to a coffee shop. She noticed that he passed several establishments that also served coffee, only stopping at the one on the opposite side of town.

Once they were seated inside with their coffee, he asked her questions about her life, about her school and what her plans for the future were.

Tabitha answered him, feeling special as this man, who was much older than the usual boys her father arranged to accompany her to different events, talked to her, got her to open up more than she'd ever spoken to another human being. The afternoon was fading into evening when she reluctantly admitted that she needed to get home.

He drove her to her house, but wouldn't release her until she promised to meet him the next day for lunch. She gladly accepted, feeling her heart race in anticipation. "Wear pants tomorrow. I make no promises on my gentlemanly behavior if you wear a skirt again," he said, smiling that wicked smile down at her again before zooming off down the road.

That night, she dreamed about Nikolai and his amazing smile, her mind wondering what his kiss would be like. She wanted to experience the touch of his lips and feel his body with her fingertips. She blushed in the darkness of her room, terrified that someone might hear her thoughts and admonish her for being so brazen.

Her father smiled at her in the morning as she came down to breakfast, an apology in his eyes as he poured her tea. "I'm terribly sorry about yesterday, Tabby," he said, handing her the honey for her tea. "I completely forgot. Meetings, you know," he said and kissed her on the cheek. "How about if I ask Susan to make a special dinner tonight to celebrate your return?" he said as he stood up, preparing to head off to work.

"That sounds lovely," she said, smiling up at him. She knew he had a lot on his mind. It had been like this all her life and she'd accepted that he was a very busy man. He was also the wealthiest in the village and had an image to uphold, which he said was time consuming and irritating but she suspected that he thrived on the power he held in his hands due to his position as the major town employer.

The morning went by slowly but she was thrilled when she heard the motorcycle coming up the drive. Bouncing down the stairs, she was already on the front porch when he stopped.

"Hello, *bella*," he said, his eyes moving over her brown, curling hair that she'd left down today. "You look ravishing," he said as he handed her a second helmet, putting it gently on her head himself. She shivered when his hands touched her chin, connecting the strap. "Are you hungry?" he asked, smiling that million dollar smile.

"Starving," she said breathlessly.

"Good," he chuckled. "So am I," he replied. "Come along."

He drove them to a pretty spot in the country, on top of a hill that looked down on the village. Tabitha had never known this place was here and she wondered how someone who had been in the village for only one day had found the prettiest spot available. "This is lovely," she said, taking the blanket he handed her and spreading it out over the grass. "How on earth did you discover it?" she asked.

"I was riding by yesterday and saw it. I'm glad you like it," he said and placed a large picnic basket down in the middle of the blanket that had been tied to the back of his bike.

"What did you bring for lunch?" she asked.

"I don't know," he said, peering down into the contents. "Let's find out together, shall we?" he said and pulled out prettily wrapped packages. Unwrapping them, she discovered rosemary chicken, fresh fruit, pungent cheese and a bottle of wine.

"Goodness," she gasped. "This is amazing. Where did you get this meal?"

"I stayed at a little bed and breakfast last night and the owner offered to make the basket this morning. She's a very good cook, if her breakfast is any way to judge."

"Do you mean the Rosemont Inn?" Tabitha asked. "That's Ms. Betsy. She's a great cook," she replied, handing him a plate filled with food before bending down to make one for herself. "She makes beautiful wedding cakes…" Tabitha started to say only to stop self-consciously. "I mean…well, I'm sure you have no need for wedding cakes," Tabitha stuttered out, sounding silly for even bringing up such a subject.

He smiled in her direction, his eyes sparkling at her discomfiture. "You never know," he said. "Good chicken."

Tabitha blushed furiously and looked down at her plate. "Yes," she said, wishing she could think of another subject. "What do you do?" she asked, trying to come up with a casual topic.

"A little bit of everything," he replied. Nikolai watched as the beautiful woman sitting opposite him tried to hide her embarrassment. He wished she wouldn't. He was completely enchanted with her. She was stunningly pretty but he suspected she had no idea of that fact, which only increased her beauty. Her soft, blue eyes were filled with everything she was thinking and feeling. There was no artifice, he thought. Traveling in his world, he'd never met someone so honest and compassionate. Tabitha was like a breath of fresh air.

"Where do you live?" she asked.

"I travel all over the world," he said, which wasn't what she was asking. Nor was it a lie. Nikolai had houses or apartments all over the world, needing them for business purposes. If he was in one city for more than two days, it was odd. In fact, he should be in London tonight for a board meeting with one of his companies, then he was scheduled to fly to Madrid for negotiations with a potential acquisition. The next morning, he was due to be in Rome for a meeting with new suppliers.

He heard her laugh and his body reacted quickly. The soft, feminine sound made him wonder why he'd spent so much time with the women of his world. Why hadn't he found Tabitha sooner? She was so genuine, he wanted to both pull her into his arms and make love to her while at the same time, get as far away from her as possible, fearful that his connection to the world of money and power would somehow taint her sweetness and purity.

"So you work at whatever interests you and you live wherever that work takes you. Is that an accurate assessment?" she asked.

"That's a relatively accurate assessment, yes."

"It sounds exciting," she said, smiling shyly at him.

Nikolai shrugged his shoulders, already rescheduling his week so he could have dinner with her tomorrow night. "It has its moments," was all he would say.

"So what do you do when you're not working?" she asked.

Nikolai thought back to the previous weekend. "I like boating," he replied, thinking of the yacht he'd just had built. He would like to take her on it, he thought. He could have his helicopter here in twenty minutes and they could simply sail away for some private time, away from the paparazzi that seemed to be hounding him, hungry for whatever his next acquisition was going to be, either female or business. They didn't care as long as it was a juicy story.

"What else?" she asked, encouraging him to talk.

He looked across the blanket at her. "I think about how much I want to kiss you," he said and was rewarded with her mouth forming a sweet little "O" and her eyes widening.

She cleared her throat and sat up straighter and Nikolai almost laughed out loud. She was interested all right. She was trying to hide her reaction but he could see her nipples peak against the white cotton shirt she was wearing. He kept his eyes upwards, not wanting to give away her body's reaction if she wasn't aware of it already.

He almost groaned with his next thought. Good grief, was this enchantingly seductive woman a virgin? His body was on fire for her but if she was a virgin, he would not touch her, he vowed.

But thirty minutes later, their lunch cleared up, she was sitting primly on her knees, answering more of his questions, laughing sweetly at his teasing and he simply couldn't help himself. She was just too beautiful and more tempting than any man should be asked to refrain from touching.

Tabitha sat on the blanket, her palms itching with the need to find out what it would be like to kiss him. Had she only imagined his comment earlier? If not, why wasn't he moving toward her? She'd been on enough dates to know that men usually found some sort of awkward, irritating way to make a move. But this man simply laid back on the blanket, laughing up at her and talking in his sexy, seductive deep voice that formed images in her mind of him talking in bed.

"Come here, Tabitha," Nikolai said, his voice now husky and his eyes hooded as he watched her face flush with anticipation.

"What?" she asked.

"Come closer," he said.

Tabitha looked down at her hands and bit her lip. "Nikolai, I don't..."

He sat up and looked into her eyes. "I promise I only want to kiss you," he said softly, reassuring her.

Tabitha was so relieved that he wasn't asking more of her, knowing that she wanted more but wasn't able to understand exactly what that "more" might be. Oh, she knew the technicalities of the sexual act, but nothing in her experience could prepare her for Nikolai.

Instead of worrying more, she simply threw herself into his arms, feeling only slightly embarrassed by his grunt when she landed on his chest. But his strong arms controlled her awkward fall and gently rolled her onto her back, his mouth slowly descending toward hers.

As soon as his lips touched hers, Tabitha knew that she was in trouble. She inhaled sharply as the heat stole through her body, her hands shaking as she touched his cheek with one, while the other tangled into his hair. When his mouth moved slowly over hers, tingles of pleasure surged into her system, and her hands brought him down, closer to her.

Over and over again, his mouth slanted across hers, his hands moving along her waist, her ribs and her hips while her body moved, begging for more as his mouth taught hers how to share the experience. "Put your tongue in my mouth," he instructed hoarsely. When she did that, his body surged upwards. She imitated whatever he did, feeling desire stoke through her body and arching her back. When his hand touched her breast, she cried out as the pleasure became so intense she had trouble controlling her reaction.

Nikolai held her tightly in his arms, allowing her to come down off the desire slowly. He whispered in her ear, his hand stroking her back as she came back to reality.

Burying her face in his chest, "I'm sorry," she said lamely.

"For what?" Nikolai asked, rolling her back so he was looking down at her.

"I don't understand what you do to me," she said, still trying to catch her breath.

"It's desire and I guarantee that it is mutual," he said, his hand reaching down to bring her hips closer to his.

Tabitha gasped when she felt the hard evidence of his erection against her thigh. Her worried eyes moving up to look into his. "Why?"

"Don't question it," he said tenderly. "Just enjoy it," and he bent to gently touch her lips again, taking her shiver of excitement into his body, thrilled that she was so incredibly responsive.

Dinner that evening was tense and boring as her father ranted and raved about problems at MacComber Industries. Susan, the housekeeper, had gone above and beyond with her culinary efforts, fixing a delicious supper for her homecoming. But she doubted that her father tasted any of the delicious roast or savory potatoes. He was too angry and frustrated with the problems cropping up at the factory and with clients.

The following evening, Tabitha met Nikolai at a small restaurant, his appearance again taking her breath away as he stood up in a pair of khakis and a white cotton shirt as she entered, then pulled out the chair for her. She was wearing a yellow sundress that hugged her figure, then flared out softly at her hips. She saw the admiration in his eyes as soon as she walked into the restaurant and was glad that she'd put so much effort into her appearance.

She had no idea what she ate that night, only that Nikolai made her laugh, respected her opinions and even encouraged her to find a job and stand up to her father. She was thrilled that he didn't think women's sole purpose in life was to be married and pregnant. But she was even more thrilled when he took her hand after dessert and led her to his motorcycle. He drove them back up into the hills so they could watch the lights twinkling in the valley. Within moments, he pulled her into his arms, kissing her senseless but this time, going one step further, his hands touching her breasts, kissing her neck and nibbling on her ear. Tabitha heard her breathing, rapid and out of control. In the distance, she heard a small animal moaning softly but was unaware that it was her own moans and gasps as Nikolai took her higher, the desire spiking through her system as he touched her in different places.

She was unaware of anything, just desperate to feel him, to hold him and do everything he was doing to her. But when he pulled her underwear off, she was almost mindless with desire. He pulled her back onto his motorcycle, only this time, she was facing him. His hands skimmed her dress, underneath, his fingers hot and his mouth hotter. When his fingers found the wet core of her being, she almost splintered into millions of pieces. But then his fingers started moving, touching her, flicking a sensitive spot and then moving again, she almost screamed out as the pleasure built, reaching almost pain as she arched her back, her hands gripping his shoulders, her nails digging into his muscles. She could barely breathe as he pulled her hips closer, spreading her legs wider, giving him greater access. Tabitha didn't care, she was mindless at this point and willing to do anything he told her to do as long as he continued to touch her that way.

When the desire got to be too much, her head thrashed back and forth and she almost started crying. "Please, Nik. You've got to stop!" she cried out, her hands reaching down to pull his fingers away. But he wouldn't let her. His other hand slipped inside her dress which had been unbuttoned, his fingers touching her now bare nipple and the double assault was too much. Her mind splintered just as her body did and she cried out, biting on his shoulder as she reached her first orgasm.

Again, Nikolai held her close, whispering things in Greek she didn't understand but she couldn't let go of him, her arms wrapped around his shoulder as her body slowly floated down to earth.

When she was able to focus once again, she looked up, directly into his dark, passion drugged eyes. Her mouth was still open and she shook her head slightly. "I never knew," she started to say. When she saw his smile broaden, she buried her face in his shoulder, embarrassed beyond belief at what she'd allowed him to do to her.

"Don't hide your reactions from me, *agape mou*," he said and pulled back, looking into her soft, blue eyes once again. "I want to see it all, every time I touch you."

She was suddenly conscious of the bulge in his slacks and was grateful for the darkness which hid her pink cheeks. "What about you?" she asked, licking her dry lips and wondering if she could give him the same amount of pleasure, but not sure what to do.

"Don't worry about me."

"But…'" she started to say but his lips covered hers, silencing her protest.

The next three days were the most magical of Tabitha's life. Thursday, they went for a hike in the woods, talking about politics and the latest books. Tabitha was astounded that the man was so well read and she discovered that he spoke five languages fluently. She never questioned why he appeared to be a drifter, fearful that he would be offended and leave. She asked him for his resume, offering to put it in to her father's company so he could find a position within the organization. Tabitha was powerfully disappointed when he simply smiled, not committing to her suggestion. She ignored the stab of pain she felt around her heart, knowing that the only reason she suggested the idea was so he might find a home in the village. At that moment, she made the decision that she would simply take whatever he could give her and live in the moment. Whatever time he was here would be enough.

By Friday though, the shoe dropped and he delivered the news that had her gasping for air as the pain sliced through her body.

"I have to leave," Nikolai said as they sat on a log, her back against his chest and his strong arms securely around her waist while his chin rested on her shoulder.

Tabitha immediately stiffened but he wouldn't let her pull away. "Why?" she asked, the fear and pain apparent in her voice. "Why can't you just stay?"

"Because I have things to do. People rely on me. I've been away too long already," he explained with his deep, sexy voice.

She'd known this time would come but she had no idea how much it would hurt. The tears immediately started falling and she turned her face around so he couldn't see them. "I understand," she said, her voice trembling.

Nikolai turned her back around, relentlessly forcing her to face him. Looking down into her tear filled eyes, he smiled gently. "Come with me," he said.

Tabitha looked up at him sharply. "What?"

"Come with me. Marry me and be my wife. I'll take care of you and I promise you'll never want for anything," he said softly.

Hope flared inside her heart and she threw her arms around his shoulders. "Are you serious? You want to marry me?"

His handsome smile made the butterflies dance around in her stomach. "Yes. I know you don't want to be married and pregnant, but I promise you'll never regret becoming my wife. We don't have to have children immediately. You can find your career. Just do it with me instead of alone."

Tabitha could barely breathe but for a completely different reason now. She was so deliriously happy she could hardly believe it. "Yes!" she said. "Oh, yes! I don't care where we go as long as we can be together," she cried between hiccups, her arms tightening around his neck. She was thrilled when he lifted her into his arms, holding her closely.

After several long minutes when she thoroughly enjoyed his kiss, his hands holding her against his hard length, he stopped suddenly and took a deep breath. "I'll need to speak with your father. When will he be available?" he asked, pulling back to look down into her expressive blue eyes that were still filled with tears. His thumb caught one as it slipped from her lash to her soft cheek. "I assume these are tears of happiness?"

"Yes," she laughed and threw her arms back around his neck. "Oh, Nikolai! I can't believe this is happening! I love you so much. I know it has only been a week but you make me feel things I never thought were possible. I've never felt this way before about anyone I've dated."

"And your father?" he asked again, laughing at her enthusiasm but he silently felt the same way about her.

That reminder doused her happiness only minimally. Her father definitely wouldn't approve of Nik's career choices, or lack of them. But she also knew that, once her father got to know Nikolai, he would love him just as much as she did. There was no doubt in her mind. "Oh! Yes." She pulled back and considered what she knew of her father's schedule. "Well, I guess he'll be available tonight although he is having some clients come by. And then he's going away for the weekend. He's been under a lot of stress lately but I'm not sure exactly why," she explained.

"Perhaps business is not going as well as normal?" Nik suggested, knowing that was actually the case. He had seen the slow decline of the stock prices over the past few days and had dug a little deeper into the issues. He had never thought about asking a father for a woman's hand in marriage but he knew how to run a business, had been the driving force behind his family's shipping empire for the past ten years and had more than doubled the vast Andretti holdings, expanding into manufacturing and inland distribution, making the entire business more efficient and powerful. He kept his suspicions about her father's business to himself, not wanting to concern Tabitha if her father had it under control.

She shrugged, unsure of what was happening at her father's factory. "I don't know. I'm sure it's something crazy, but he's always been able to pull through these things in the past."

Nikolai didn't want to voice his doubts about that at this time. Once they were married, he would offer his assistance to her father, perhaps pull him out of what Nikolai suspected was a very deep and expensive hole. "Come, let's get this over with so we can start planning the wedding," he said, taking hold of her hand and guiding her back to his motorcycle.

When they arrived at the house five minutes later, it was to see her father shaking hands with another man. Tabitha had seen the shorter man on several occasions but had stayed out of the way, knowing that her father was working on what she sensed was a very sensitive business deal with him.

Tabitha was only slightly nervous when they rode up, noticing that her father's eyes narrowed at the motorcycle and leather jacket. Good grief, she thought to herself, her father acted like this was the nineteen sixties and a leather jacket immediately spelled trouble.

"Tabitha! Where have you been all afternoon?" he demanded as soon as the engine was turned off. "Lucy Munroe has been calling, asking for help with her bridesmaid's dress."

"Really?" Tabitha said, confused by both his abruptness at her appearance and his obvious rudeness in front of Nikolai. Tabitha was surprised that her father hadn't waited for an introduction to Nik before firing off a comment like that. Being the owner of the largest business in the village, Edward MacComber was intensely aware of appearances and went out of his way to be polite even to the church gardener. It was also odd that Lucy was worried about the bridesmaid's dress she was wearing to her brother's wedding this weekend. Tabitha had seen Lucy try it on a couple of days earlier and it was fine.

"Yes. I suspect that you should head over there immediately to see what is going on," he continued. "Dresses can be tricky things, you know. And everything has to look perfect for weddings. Don't they?" The words were spoken to Tabitha, but she suspected that they were actually directed at Nik for some reason. Her father was acting very odd.

Tabitha looked up at Nik and shook her head. "But, Father, I think Nikolai needs to discuss something with you. It is rather important." She was trying to hide the happiness she was currently feeling but knew that some of it was coming out in her expression.

The color in Edward's face drained away and he harrumphed quickly. "I suspect that whatever this man needs to talk to me about does not require your attention. So go along," he said in a patronizing voice. "See what you can do to help Lucy with her dress while I discuss whatever it is this man wants to discuss with me."

Without another word, Edward walked into the house, leaving the front door open to allow Nik to either follow or not, uncaring about either eventuality.

Tabitha looked up at Nik, an apology already on her lips but he put a finger to stop her. "Go along to help your friend. I'll speak to your father and I'll see you when you are through," he said, giving her a gentle kiss before moving off with confidence to the front door.

A tingle of fear went through her body for a moment, but she banished it, knowing that Nik of all people would be able to overcome any arguments her father might have. And even if he couldn't, Tabitha was too happy about starting a life with Nik. She would leave her father's house if he didn't approve of her marriage. She was in love and, although she knew love wouldn't put food on the table, she was confident enough that they would never starve. She wasn't afraid of being poor. She was more afraid of living without Nik than anything else.

She rushed off hurriedly, wanting to find out what Lucy had called about so she could quickly come back to Nik and start making plans.

After watching Tabitha walk through the immaculate yard, entranced by her simple grace and elegance, Nik followed Tabitha's father into the house. Nik assumed the man would find some position of strength, which is exactly how he would treat this situation. Nik was struck by the idea of a common bond with Edward. Knowing that he wanted to have children with Tabitha, possibly a girl, he could understand, to a point, where Edward's animosity was coming from. He wouldn't like giving up his daughter to a stranger, someone who had never been properly introduced to his family. Nor would his family allow it.

Having that insight, Nik found Edward in the man's office. "Good afternoon, sir. I'd like to introduce myself," he said, reaching out to offer his hand to the older man. "I'm Nikolai Andretti," he said, as if that would be enough.

"Forget all these niceties," Edward growled rudely, ignoring Nik's outstretched hand as he sat back in his large, leather chair and lit a cigar, not bothering to offer Nik one. "How much will it take to get rid of you? And don't be too greedy. Despite the nice, large house and owning my own company, I'm pretty stretched for cash right now."

Nik's face hardened with contempt. The man actually thought Nik could be bought? The man didn't have enough money in his bank account to buy an Andretti. There wasn't enough money in the world, he thought to himself. He tempered his anger, reminding himself that the man was Tabitha's father. "I don't think you understand," Nik started again, knowing he'd have to explain further. "I'm not asking for money. I just want your daughter's hand in marriage."

Hearing the words, Edward exploded out of his chair, his cigar precariously dangling from his round fingers as his anger took over, making his face red and his eyes look like they could pop out of their sockets at any moment. "Are you out of your mind? There's no way in hell I'd let my daughter marry a loser like you. My daughter has class and elegance. She's beautiful dammit! And you have the audacity to come here and think you're good enough for her? I don't think you have the right to clean her shoes!"

Something in Nik's expression must have shown Edward that his intimidation tactics were not going to work on Nik and he abruptly changed, visibly forcing himself to calm down and return to his desk and leather chair. "Besides, she's already engaged. I'm not sure what she's been telling you for the past week, but she's scheduled to be married in two weeks. That's one of the reasons I'm so strapped for cash right now. The dammed wedding is the talk of the town and every one plus their mother is coming around to finally see my daughter get married. The plans have already been made, dress picked out and even the cake ordered. Why the hell do you think Lucy needs help with a bridesmaid's dress? Tabitha wants everything perfect for her wedding. Not a flower out of place!" He puffed slightly on his cigar, watching Nik through a cloud of smoke. "So tell me, what did she say or do to convince you that she was available?" his mocking smile enraging Nik almost as much as his words had.

Nik placed his hands on his hips and shook his head. All thoughts about the past week were prancing through his mind and everything he knew about Tabitha told him that this man was lying. "I don't believe you. Your daughter is not that kind of a woman."

Edward laughed heartily. "You think so? Want to know how many men she's had offers of marriage from? Men have tick marks for each woman he beds. Tabitha, I'm ashamed to say, makes tick marks for each proposal of marriage she's managed to elicit from the men of this town." His eyes narrowed and he puffed during the silence. "What did she promise you? That she'd be willing to live in poverty with you? That she wanted only you and you're the only man who's touched her?"

Nik's mind was whirling. He'd only known Tabitha for less than a week. His instincts were telling him that this man was lying to him. But why would he do that? He obviously didn't know the Andretti name or he would definitely be singing a different tune. Every momma from London to Greece, and probably even beyond, had been trying to marry off their eligible daughters to Nik ever since he came of age in the hopes of tapping in to the Andretti billions as well as the prestige and power that came along with that wealth.

Edward chuckled, moving in for the kill. "Forget about her. And don't worry about her at all. I can guarantee that my daughter will stop her teasing in two weeks. Her new husband has been forgiving enough but he won't allow her to continue her chase after their wedding. He'll be very demanding of her time and attention. So why don't you head on out to your next stop on the road and charm some other woman? Tabitha will have forgotten about you by the time she gets back from Lucy's house. Have no fears. In fact, she'll probably be grateful to me for getting rid of you so easily. Tabitha doesn't really like to do her dirty work."

Nik stood there for another long moment, wanting to challenge him but unable to do so. It was entirely possible that Tabitha was stringing him along. He remembered the odd looks from some of the town's people as they'd eaten at various places. At the time, he'd simply assumed that the looks were due to him being a stranger out with their local beauty. But it made more sense that the looks were due to an imminent wedding that everyone was involved in planning.

And he couldn't discount the nights she said she'd have to be home with her family. Had that actually been the nights she was with her fiancé? He'd never been invited home, despite the fact Tabitha suspected that he didn't work during the day. She'd mentioned once that she liked having him as a secret. How much of a secret was he really? At the time, he'd been amused by the idea since he too had been keeping their relationship a secret, enjoying dating a woman without the paparazzi trailing his every move and photographing him, speculating on the newest woman's romantic powers over him and the potential for a marriage proposal. This week had been a novel period in his life. But had it been simply fantasy?

The feelings Tabitha had stirred within him had not been fantasy, but perhaps the idea of love for him was just that, unreal and never would be. A stab of pain sliced through his gut at that idea.

"Mull those little tidbits around in that good-looking brain of yours," Edward said jovially. "If it's any consolation, I'll let you in on the fact that you're probably the most handsome man she's dallied with. Most of them are a little less....manly," he said, chuckling at some sort of joke that only he knew about.

Nik stiffened, accepting that the man was telling the truth about Tabitha. Nik could think of no reason a father would say such vile things about his daughter unless they were true. "I see. Well, in that case, I'll see myself out. Please explain to Tabitha that I am glad that I was at least her most 'manly' suitor," Nik said. He bowed slightly, a mocking salutation to the man who had raised such a promiscuous daughter.

Nik walked out into the bright sunshine, stunned that the world still looked exactly as it had only thirty minutes ago, yet at the same time, it looked bleaker, more sinister. And definitely less forgiving.

Climbing on his motorcycle, he revved the engine and, without a backwards look or even putting on his helmet, Nik drove off, heading back to London. As soon as he had the small town's outskirts behind him, he pulled out his cell phone as he recklessly turned the corner, barely pulling out in time to avoid colliding with a wall of rock to the left of the road. Calling his PA, he ordered the helicopter to get into the air and find him along the highway. He knew the helicopter was able to land in just about any field and he could be back at work within fifteen minutes versus the hour long ride to London via motorcycle. He was due in Milan tomorrow and there was a family gathering the next day.

With a determined expression on his face, he considered all the activities he could use to distract him from this week and erase his foolish behavior from his mind.

He was used to working eighteen hour days but after the week with Tabitha, he pushed his staff harder, sometimes working straight through the night and into the next day. He saw the news of Tabitha's wedding by accident in the papers and all of his anger increased as he read the evidence of Edward's words. That afternoon, the crushed newspaper by his side, he stopped all negotiations with a particularly difficult acquisition and, within two days, he had accomplished through merciless business tactics what several months of negotiations would have done. That was the point when his enemies started quivering when he entered the room and even his friends began to hide. No one crossed Nik after that takeover.

An hour after leaving Nik, Tabitha was running happily back across the lawn, sure that the conversation with her father was finished and she'd be able to throw herself into his arms and experience the blissful feelings only he could show her. Her steps faltered when she didn't see the motorcycle still in the front. Rushing into the house, she called out for her father. She eventually found him in his room pulling on his suit jacket. "Father? What happened?" she asked, a smile forming across her face since she couldn't hide the happiness she was feeling

Edward looked down at his daughter, then his eyes slid away. "He's gone," was all he said.

Tabitha laughed joyfully, unconcerned despite his gruff, almost angry disposition. Nothing could bother her now, knowing that she and Nik would be together. "I know he's gone. His motorcycle was gone from the driveway. But aren't you happy for me?" she asked, clasping her hands together and almost jumping up and down in excitement.

Edward straightened the cuffs of his suit jacket and shook his head. "No. He's gone. I kicked him out of the house."

That stunned Tabitha but she still didn't understand. "But why?" she asked, some of her happiness fading. "Why on earth would you do something like that? Please don't tell me you were rude to him."

Edward's face turned red at Tabitha's admonition and his eyes sharpened as he turned fully toward his daughter. "Rude? The man comes in here and tells me he wants to take you away? And you don't think I have a right to be rude to the arrogant bastard? Of course I was rude. And if he ever shows his face in this town again, I'll make sure he's arrested and dragged down the street in chains! No daughter of mine is going to be used by a drifter with no prospects and no future!"

Tabitha started shaking her head in denial midway through his explosion. "No father! You misunderstood. He wants to marry me!"

Edward puffed up, his face almost turning purple. "Marriage! I don't think so, Tabitha. Marriage was never brought up today. In fact, exactly the opposite! The man only wants your body and said you'd been a perfect tease for the past week. What do you think I am supposed to say about something so awful! A father will never allow his daughter to be used like that."

Tabitha cringed at her father's words but shook her head, denying the possibility that Nik would say such things. He was a gentleman. He would never reveal the things they had done together. Not to anyone! "No, really! You misunderstood! He's not like that. He's extremely intelligent and we'll find some way to live happily."

"The man's a womanizer!' he shouted back. "Can't you see that he just goes from one woman to another, demanding money in exchange for leaving them alone?" His angry tirade became even angrier. "I wouldn't pay him a dime and that angered him. Even if he was serious about marrying you, which he wasn't, there is no way I would let my only daughter marry a drifter! He's nothing. He's one of those people we support with our tax dollars because they live off society. I'm not allowing my daughter to marry someone who can't even support himself, and wouldn't allow you to live in the lifestyle to which you deserve. No, Tabitha. That marriage is not happening. Not over my dead body!"

Tabitha was already sobbing at his hurtful words. "You're wrong about Nik. He's not like that. He was sincere about marrying me and he'd never go on to another woman! We're in love and I'm going to find him and tell him that I don't care about your approval. He won't either."

Edward whipped his half smoked cigar out of his mouth, pointing it at her as he yelled, "Bite your tongue young lady! I forbid you to contact that man and I've told him that already. You won't be hearing from him ever again!" He turned away from her and stared out the window, dismissing Tabitha and accepting that she would bend to his will. All people bowed down to whatever he decreed. It was the way this village worked and he would accept nothing less from his daughter.

Tabitha ran out of the room and up to her bedroom, terrified of his words. She immediately picked up her cell phone and called Nik's mobile number but he didn't answer it. Nor did he answer the phone for the next several days, leaving Tabitha to start to question his sincerity. As much as she fought against her doubts, the longer it took her to reach him, the more the insidious thoughts invaded her psyche. She hated that, wanted desperately to believe that what they'd felt for each other was real and lasting. But as the days passed by, she wondered if his feelings for her had been sincere.

She avoided her father completely, staying in her room until she was sure he had gone for the day, then making sure she had something to do outside the house for the evening, not coming home until late. Sometimes it meant she would stay at the library, hiding in the stacks and staring at a book, her tortured mind unable to absorb any of the words on the pages. Other times, she would be with friends, but only in a physical sense. Her thoughts were constantly wondering about Nik; where he was, what he was doing and upper most in her list of questions, why had he left her like this with no word?

One evening while lying in bed, once again unable to sleep, she simply stared up at the ceiling, the tears silently falling to dampen her pillow. Desperate, she sat up and grabbed her mobile, dialing Nik's number once again. It was almost midnight and she'd tried so many times that day to reach Nik on the phone but without success. She was phoning him one last time that night in the hopes that she could reach him before bed. On the fifth ring, Tabitha's heart soared. "Nik?" she called out as the phone was finally answered instead of going to voice mail.

"Who's this?" a sultry, female voice asked.

Tabitha's heart plummeted. "Is this Nik's phone?" she asked, hoping she'd just had the wrong phone number all this time and that the woman with the sexy voice owned the phone instead of Nik. She hated the idea that her father could be right about Nik's character.

Unfortunately, her dreams were about to crash yet again. "Yes, it is. Who is calling?" the female demanded. Tabitha heard laughter and music in the background.

The words her father had spoken just a few days ago came back to her. Were they true? Was Nik already on to the next woman? The idea stabbed through her stomach, leaving her gasping for breath. "No one," she said miserably. "Just forget that I called."

Two days later, Tabitha didn't hear the knock that sounded on her door as she sat on her bed, staring off at the wall. She couldn't cry, couldn't think. She was in too much pain to even care when her father walked in without waiting for her to reply.

"Tabitha! What are you doing lying around?" he demanded angrily. He was dressed, as usual, in a business suit but his hair was slightly more rumpled, as if he'd been running his fingers through it recently.

She didn't even bother to answer him, continuing to simply stare at the wall.

Her lack of response didn't bother him in the least. "Well, never mind that. I don't really care anyway. Here's the issue. You wanted to get married, so I've found you a husband," he stated roughly. "The man is very well connected and will maintain the standard of living you're used to."

No response.

"You'll be married next week, since I understand you're in an all-fired hurry to start married life," he explained.

Still, no response.

"I'll have Lydia start on your wedding dress," he said gruffly and walked out, slamming the door behind him.

One week later, Tabitha somehow found herself in front of the village minister saying her vows to the man who had been in the driveway that awful afternoon when Nik had left her. She didn't care if she married the stranger, uncaring about anything after Nik's betrayal. She'd trusted him, fell in love with him and finding out that he was nothing like the man she'd thought he was had been too painful. She didn't trust her own instincts so why not marry her father's choice?

Reality hit harder than she had expected. As far as she knew, the wedding went off without a hitch although she was unaware of anything around her. Even the kiss after the vows did nothing to break her out of her misery.

It wasn't until the honeymoon started that night that the horror of her marriage was to arrive and break through her depression. She nervously changed into a silk negligee, banishing the thought that she wished Nik could see her like this and swallowing her revulsion at the idea of her new husband, a virtual stranger, would be touching her the way Nik had touched her so many weeks ago. She hated the idea, but love hadn't worked out for her. This was her lot in life, she assumed sadly.

Walking into the luxurious hotel room that was to be their first stop on a two week long vacation, she stood in the doorway, horror dawning on her face as she watched her groom in the process of making love to his best man.

"Get out!" she heard him yell at her. Tabitha didn't wait for another warning, she spun on her heel and slammed the bathroom door, terrified of what she'd seen and heard. Shaking in misery, she sank down on to the bathroom floor, her mind whirling at how her life had become one painful nightmare after another.

She slept on the bathroom floor that night, crying herself to sleep and unaware that she'd actually slept until her husband nudged her with his toe the following morning. "We're leaving," was all he said before stepping into the shower naked.

The two weeks in a Caribbean resort were not as bad. Knowing that they would be spending more time together, her husband, Jerry, had booked a two bedroom suite. She stayed by herself, angry and terrified of anyone discovering that her husband preferred a man to herself.

Once back home, living in the man's house, she found that he had an angry temper.

"I'm leaving," she said as soon as they walked into the house she was supposed to live in with him.

"Where are you going?" he snarled.

She shivered in revulsion at the man standing in front of the door, hindering her departure. "I don't know. But I'm not staying in this marriage or this house anymore. I'll get an annulment and I'll find my own place to live," she said, moving toward the garage door since he obviously wasn't going to let her leave through the front.

He grabbed her by her arm and swung her around. "Don't even think about it," he snapped. "You leave and your father's business goes down the drain. He's in a lot of trouble financially and, let's just say I'm helping him out of the mess he's made of the business."

"What are you talking about?" she demanded, her eyes widening at his accusation.

He sneered at her shocked expression a moment before his eyes dropped down her body. "I mean, your father is a complete failure at running that boring little factory he inherited. He needed someone to lead him out of the pit the business had fallen into. And I needed someone to act as my hostess and make sure the gossips don't continue with their accusations and assumptions about my sexual preferences. I can't do business in this small town with people thinking I'm more into men than women." His eyes sliced down her figure again. "And you fit the bill perfectly," he sneered. "All those rumors are gone now that you're supposedly sharing my bed. So just sit pretty and everything will be fine. Make any move to leave, and I'll demand all the money back from your father."

"I don't believe you! My father's business is not in financial trouble, much less bankrupt if that's what you are implying. He's a financial genius and can fix just about anything."

"Ask him," Jerry replied, smiling mercilessly.

Tabitha did just that and was stunned to hear her father confirm Jerry's statement.

Jerry died in a car accident six months after her wedding so before she could figure out how to save the factory and get out of her marriage, the nightmare was over. Her father died of a heart attack two months later. Despite the painful previous nine months, Tabitha stepped into her father's shoes at that point and cut costs, energized the staff by reassuring everyone that she would find an adequate replacement as the head of the company, someone with vigor and drive that would hold MacComber Industries together and take it into the next one hundred years. She remained on as one of the board of directors, but knew she didn't have the experience to run the company. She nominated one of the vice presidents, Nelson, to step in and run the company.

Coming back to the present, she realized she hadn't eaten any of her frozen meal and it was now just a congealed mess on the plastic, microwaveable tray. She threw it into the trash and thought about the three years since her father's death. The rest, she thought miserably as she wiped her hands and left the kitchen, was history.

In bed that night, Tabitha looked out the window of her bedroom and forced her mind to stop dwelling on the past. She picked up the business card again and looked down at the number. She had to reach out to him and somehow convince him that he'd be hurting an entire village with his course of action.

Calling the phone number listed on the card, her fingers shook as she brought the receiver to her ear. He answered on the second ring and her hand tightened in fear and something else she didn't want to identify.

"Hello?" the deep voice answered.

"Nikolai?" Tabitha asked, hoping her voice didn't sound scared to his ears.

"Yes Tabitha. Have you come to a decision?" he asked casually, as if he couldn't care less one way or the other which answer she gave him.

Taking a deep breath to steady her nerves, she forced her mind to move forward, knowing she had to convince him that this was not good for either of them. "Well, I wanted to talk to you about that."

There was a moment of silence. "I didn't think this would be a hard equation for someone of your intellect to work through. You're a smart woman, Tabitha, if a little loose on the morals side of things," he said.

Tabitha gasped, "Why, you arrogant bastard! I can't believe someone with your history with women could possibly call me loose!"

"Didn't you sell yourself to your dead husband? Basically, you're doing the same thing now. Is the price so much different?" he asked.

He couldn't know anything about her marriage! "No! That was a completely different arrangement," she said, humiliated at the mere mention of her horrible marriage.

"Ah, you're a hypocrite as well, eh?" he chuckled. "I'm not sure you understand the true impact of this situation, Tabitha. If you don't come to me tomorrow afternoon with the right answer, you're company will no longer exist. The same thing happened right before you sold yourself to Jerry Manning. I understand immediately after your wedding, there was a significant influx of cash to MacComber Industries. You, in fact, saved your father's company from going under. Just think of this as being the same thing, which, in fact, it is."

"It isn't," she stated emphatically. She knew there'd been an exchange of funds but she couldn't dwell on that humiliation, so she focused on what she didn't understand. "You can't really expect me to go through with this, do you?"

"I think we should discuss this tomorrow over lunch," he said smoothly. "I'll meet you at my office at twelve o'clock sharp. If you're not there, I'll assume you've turned down my offer and will begin the sales. I already have three potential buyers in line for the parts to the factory." There was a long pause before he said softly, "Don't let me down, Tabitha."

Tabitha dropped the receiver as if were on fire, then buried her face in her hands. He knew! How could he possibly know about her terrible marriage? Did he know everything? Could he know that Jerry had had no interest in her? That just the thought of touching her made him cringe? Their entire six month marriage had been a sham put on for society and to this day, she remained untouched, disgusted whenever any man wanted to touch her.

Men were horrible, vile creatures, she reminded herself. The one man she had trusted with all her heart had broken her trust and her faith. She moved from that terrible relationship to a man who couldn't stand her. To this day, she refused all dates, fearing that she was simply cursed when it came to relationships. And now here was further proof.

But how could she go to him tomorrow? He would discover her secret and she would be humiliated all over again. Two men in her life – neither of whom really wanted to touch her. Well, Nik wanted to touch her but he also wanted the freedom to move on to the next woman before he said goodbye to her.

Chapter 4

Tabitha smoothed her skirt and held her purse in her hands, afraid Nik might see that her hands were shaking if she didn't have something to hold. Walking up to the security desk at ten minutes to twelve was the most terrifying moment of her life.

She had no choice. During the hour long drive to London this morning, she'd debated back and forth, coming up with one argument after another. Did she have a chance to persuade him to change his mind? Maybe – if she were extremely convincing, she could tell him about the people who depended on the company. People who had dedicated their lives to MacComber Industries and didn't deserve to be pawns in a rich man's revenge.

The security guard standing sentry in the lobby of Nik's office building politely handed her a plastic badge, then directed her to a private elevator in the back of the lobby. Within moments, she was walking down the thick carpeting of the hallway toward a set of double doors. The halls were quiet but people were rushing about quickly, efficiently, as if they all had an urgent purpose. Meanwhile, she dragged her feet slowly, unwilling to rush to her execution.

When she reached the doors, a smart, efficient looking woman in a brown tweed suit and gray hair smiled at her. "Ms. MacComber, Mr. Andretti will only be a moment. If you'll have a seat, I'll let him know you are waiting." She waved her hand toward an elegant sitting area right outside a set of double doors.

Tabitha nodded and felt as if she'd been given a small reprieve. Taking a seat on one of the long, comfortable looking sofas, she closed her eyes and focused on breathing in and out. This had to be the most convincing argument she'd ever make in her life. If she failed…Tabitha shuddered, unwilling to consider the repercussions.

"Meditation?" a deep voice chuckled.

Tabitha's eyes flashed open and she stared up into the amused face of Nikolai. Had she thought he was handsome in jeans and a leather jacket? Today, in this ultra-modern environment with a black suit and red, silk tie, the man was devastatingly gorgeous. Her body, remembering only the desire his hands were able to evoke within her, was starting to tremble. A response was needed, but her mind simply refused to work. She could only stare up at him.

One eyebrow raised in question, "I'm sure you have something to say to me but perhaps it would be more appropriately discussed in my office versus here in the reception area?"

His calm demeanor somehow snapped Tabitha out of her reverie and she stood up quickly, her purse dropping to the floor. Thankfully, nothing spilled out but as she bent to pick it up, her skirt rose up higher on her thighs, revealing a good bit of her legs before she could stand up and cover herself again.

"Wasn't that the way this whole thing started?" he asked, reminding her of the afternoon she rode on his motorcycle in a skirt.

Gasping, she pushed down the material quickly, her face heating up with embarrassment. Was there no end to how this man could torment her?

"I would think that those memories would be pushed out of your mind by now. They certainly have for me," she said and brushed passed him through the open doorway.

She heard the door close behind her and shivered.

"What's your answer?" he asked, walking casually to lean against his desk and watching her as she looked out over the city of London.

Nik watched in fascination as she debated silently with herself on how to start the conversation. Her shoulders sagged slightly before she found some inner core of strength. Turning to face him, he had to admire her courage. His body instantly reacted, hardening painfully and all he wanted to hear was her answer. He knew it would be the right one. He remembered talking to her four years ago and she had so much pride in her little village, laughing about the foibles of some of the members but also trying hard to convince him about their good sides as well. At the time, he'd thought she was quaint.

Now, knowing that all of his efforts depended on whether she had been faking that feeling too, he tensed.

"I wanted to appeal to your better nature," she said, forcing a smile on her face. "You might not respect women very much but I'm hoping you respect hard working employees and their families."

"Who says I don't respect women?"

She blinked at his interruption. "I do. You can't treat women the way you treated me all those years ago and then expect me to believe that you respect them now, do you?" she asked, losing her polite mask as the anger welled up in her chest.

His face showed no emotion to either her accusation or the emotions threatening to choke her. "On the contrary. I treated you with complete respect. It was not me who sold my body to the highest bidder." His eyes turned speculative and he asked, "By the way, how did your father feel the day he realized how wealthy and powerful I was?"

"I don't think he ever...." Tabitha stopped, remembering one afternoon when she came to the house after her wedding only to hear him ranting and raving about bad choices and leather jackets.

He smiled sardonically. "I can tell from your expression that he soon regretted tossing me out of the house. But I'll let you in on a secret," he said, moving closer. "I did some digging into the company's history and found some interesting details. All of my money and power would have been useless in your father's case. He was an arrogant son of a bitch who ignored sound business advice. He was doomed from the moment he took control from your grandfather."

Tabitha gritted her teeth and considered defending her father. But in the end, she couldn't. By the time of his death, he had killed all the feelings she'd had inside her due to his callous treatment of her as simply an object to sell to another person. She didn't mention that to Nik, knowing it would only condemn her further in his eyes. And it would also raise questions about her marriage which she couldn't...wouldn't.. discuss with him.

"Let's leave my father out of this, shall we?" she said tightly.

Nik's smile increased. "I thought so," he said and shrugged. "Just goes to show you that you shouldn't judge a book by its cover."

"I never did that," she challenged.

"Didn't you?" he asked, moving closer. "Oh, I think you probably liked my attentions while you were secure in the knowledge that daddy had all the money you could possibly spend. But when it came down to living without it and marrying me, someone you thought had nothing, or marrying someone you thought could maintain your lifestyle, there really was no question, was there?"

Tabitha didn't want to reveal to him how much she had genuinely felt for him four years ago. She felt foolish now. "Let's just chalk up four years ago to inexperience and move on, shall we?"

"That's exactly what I'm willing to do. But that experience tells me that you and I will still be incredible in bed together. And I want what I denied myself all those years ago." He paused for effect. "If I'd known how cheap you were willing to sell yourself back then, I'd probably have paid the price. But now, I'm ready to gain back what I consider mine."

She didn't want to hear the answer. She told herself not to ask. But somehow, the words just slipped out. "You mean me?" She hated herself for asking once the words slipped out of her mouth.

"Of course. You sold yourself once to save the company. What's the decision this time?" he asked, moving behind his desk and shuffling through his papers.

Tabitha was furious that her decision was of so little import to him that he could easily move on to the next business deal, which of course was all he considered this situation.

Her body was practically shaking with the rage she was currently feeling. She wished she could smack his smug face and scratch his eyes out. He couldn't care less that he'd put her into an awful position. It was all about his wants and his desires, discarding the families that would be out of work and a village that would slowly shrivel up and die without the factory and the revenue it generated. "How can you sleep at night knowing that you're going to put so many people out of work? Their skills are specialized to MacComber's needs! They won't be able to find work and the whole town will die out."

Nik stopped sifting through the documents and looked right at her. "If you don't want the town to die out, then perhaps you should be at my apartment tonight and be ready for dinner. This is not my decision, Tabitha," he said firmly. "If you want to save your precious village, then agree to my terms." He looked down at his watch. "And your deadline is over. I need an answer immediately."

She shivered at the hard steel behind his voice. Her anger was replaced by panic that was so overwhelming, she was almost physically ill. "You can't mean this! You can't really be putting an ultimatum on me in this manner."

"On the contrary. I am very definitely putting this on you. What will it be? Yes or no?"

"No," she gasped, holding her purse against her chest in a defensive manner, as if the slim leather could block out is hateful words and offer.

He immediately turned around and picked up the phone. "John, go ahead with the contracts. MacComber Industries is on the market effective immediately."

"NO!" Tabitha said, rushing over and slamming her finger onto the button that would disconnect the conversation. "You can't mean that."

"It is done," he said ominously. "If you'll excuse me, I have another meeting," he said and moved around the desk toward the door.

"Wait!" she shouted, the panic almost overwhelming her.

He turned around and faced her, one eyebrow raised in inquiry.

"Fine! I'll do it," she stammered out, unsure of any alternative. She had tried to convince him, reach his better nature but apparently, the man didn't have one. "How long? When does it start? What are the terms?" she said, her face blushing at the idea of what she was about to embark upon.

In response, he walked back over to his desk and picked up the phone again. "John, hold off for now. But be on standby."

Turning to Tabitha, she shrank from the look of victory in his eyes. "You won't regret this, Tabitha. I can guarantee that you'll find me a very generous lover," he said, touching her skin, his thumb rubbing along her lower lip. "As for how long, until I tire of you. It starts immediately and the terms are that you follow all my instructions without question. When the affair is over, you'll own the company outright. You'll be able to run the company as you see fit without the interference of that tired, pathetic, old fashioned board of directors to hinder you."

She gasped, terrified of everything he said. "Now? Immediately?" Of all the words he'd just spoken, those were the only ones that registered in her foggy, panic muddled mind.

"Yes." He walked over to his desk and pressed a button. "Elaine, cancel my appointments this afternoon and call Zeth, tell him we're on our way over. Also make reservations at Anthony's for dinner."

He released the button and walked back to her. "Ready to go?"

"Go where?"

"For clothes," he said simply and put a hand to the small of her back, guiding her out of the office.

"Clothes?" she asked, feeling silly for repeating everything he said to her.

"Of course," he replied. "I don't want you dressing like that. Too conservative," he replied, looking up and down her simple black suit with the cream silk shirt underneath. "I'd like to see you in brighter colors; dresses and outfits that will enhance your looks, not cover them up," he said simply and efficiently as if this was standard operating procedures for his girlfriends and lovers. "I'll pick out a new wardrobe for you. You'll also have credit cards, but I reserve the right to reject things you purchase if they don't suit me."

"You're kidding?"

"I never kid," he said and pressed the button for the elevator which immediately appeared.

She couldn't help but ask, "Do you do this for all of the women in your life?"

They were alone in the elevator and his height gave him a scary appearance with the shadows of the dim lighting in the cab. "Of course," he said easily.

Tabitha didn't ask any other questions. She didn't want to know how he treated his other women. She hated being part of the crowd and in this case, it was a very big crowd, she suspected.

A limousine was waiting at the entrance to the building with a bulky man holding the back door open. They rode over to an exclusive boutique and Tabitha, who had always had the very best clothes in the village, was shocked at how outrageous the prices were.

They were seated in the back of the store and served tea while the manager, who was obviously named Zeth and fawned all over Tabitha, clapped his hands and a procession of women walked out, each of them wearing breathtaking gowns in every shade of the rainbow.

Tabitha sat in a satin covered chair and watched as the beautiful dresses passed by her, noting that Nik nodded several times. Suits, day dresses, bathing suits, casual outfits and sporty little short skirts were paraded in front of her. Tabitha had no idea what was going on but she could tell that Nik was buying more outfits than she'd ever owned in her life. And whereas her current wardrobe consisted of feminine but very conservative suits and day dresses, these outfits were anything but conservative. All were within good taste, but were meant to entice and enhance.

After an hour of choosing dresses, Nik stood up. "Send whatever accessories are needed for the outfits to this address," he said, handing Zeth a card, "And she'll change into that one now," he explained, pointing to a red silk dress that wrapped at the waist, forming a deep V at the neckline and flaring out at the waist to a full skirt.

"Excuse me?" Tabitha asked, staring at the incredibly beautiful model that was currently wearing the dress. "I don't think I'll look as good in that style as she does," she said warily.

"Nonsense. You'll look great in it." His eyes looked down at hers, challenging her to say no.

Tabitha considered it for all of two seconds, then thought better of it. He only wanted her in a dress. She really should save her battles for something larger. Like sex for the first time.

Sighing deeply, she went back to a dressing room. Pulling on the red silk was like changing her skin. Gone was the professional looking suit with the conservative black wool that barely skimmed her figure. The red silk clung to her breasts, actually showing a large part of her bra. One of the sales ladies smiled secretly and handed her a red silk bra that was barely anything at all. "This might work better," she said and winked conspiratorially. Tabitha took off the dress again and changed out of her bra. She was startled when a hand appeared with another piece of red lace. "Since you're wearing the bra, here is the matching pair of underwear. You will probably feel better if you're more coordinated everywhere," the voice of the sales clerk said.

Tabitha took the scrap of lace and raised it up to her eyes to determine the best way to get into them. At least it wasn't a thong, she told herself. Pulling off her sensible cotton underwear, she slipped into the lace panties and surveyed her image in the mirror. The lace covered her completely in the front, looking like a very short pair of shorts. But her bottom was uncovered slightly at the edge, as if to reveal just a taste, to tease the observer. Wearing the underwear made her feel wicked and incredibly sexy. Did she want to do that? Knowing everything that was probably going to happen tonight, she wasn't so sure. But shouldn't she prepare herself? These scraps of lace certainly gave her confidence, something severely lacking in her right at the moment.

Shrugging her shoulders, she pulled the red silk back over her shoulders and looped the long belt around her small waist, tying the bow at the side just as the model had done. When she looked up, she was surprised at how different she looked. The lace bra allowed more of her cleavage to show. It wasn't indecent, but definitely sexy. The lace of her panties didn't show through the fabric so much as made her move in a completely different way. Swirling the dress around her legs, she admired her image in the mirror.

Seeing her reflection, she wondered if Nik would think her pretty and sexy in the dress. How could he not? She smiled and Tabitha thought that even her smile had changed with the new clothes. It was more subtle but she could see the anticipation in her eyes, the hope that perhaps she was sexy? Maybe the other men in her life had been wrong and she was pretty and worthwhile?

That thought stunned her. She *wanted* Nik to find her sexy? Was she insane? He had bought her in a completely business-like fashion and she was excited about letting him see her in this dress?

Shaking her head at her completely inappropriate thoughts, she quickly folded her suit and stacked the pieces neatly in a pile, hoping the staff could send them with her new clothes to whatever address Nik had given them.

Stepping out of the dressing room, there were three sales people plus Zeth waiting to help her with anything else she might need. As soon as she saw them, she noticed four sets of eyes widen in surprise. "Is it that bad?" she asked, looking down and pulling the V on her neckline closed slightly. It didn't do any good, the silk simply fell right back to the original place where it had been hugging her breasts before the tug.

"Darling, you look smashing!" Zeth said. "I think I'm going to have to take that dress off the market. No one else will look as good in it as you so what's the point?" he said, waving his hand in the air dramatically.

The other three women nodded, smiling as if they knew some sort of secret. Zeth rushed forward, carrying a pair of red sandals in his right hand and a red purse in the other. "Here you go, Lovey!"

Tabitha pulled on the strappy red sandals and changed the contents of her black purse for the red one.

"I guess I should get out there and see how Nik likes the dress, eh?" she suggested.

"Darling, don't you worry about him. He said for you to meet him at Picolo's down the street."

"He didn't even wait for me?" Why were her feelings hurt by his action?

Zeth shook his head and laughed. "He had some call and started speaking in a language I've never heard of and took off. The car is waiting for you as well as your security detail though."

"Security detail?" she asked, sounding dazed.

"Yes. Some big, bulky guy that's been standing by the door for the past two hours and glaring at anyone who tried to walk into this dressing room."

"Oh. Well," she said, trying to find that confidence she'd discovered so briefly in the dressing room, "I guess I should be on my way to that restaurant you mentioned."

"Knock him dead!" one of the sales girls said and raised her thumb upwards.

Tabitha smiled and climbed into the back of the waiting limousine. A few minutes later, the car pulled to a stop outside a very elegant restaurant and the doorman immediately opened the back of the car. Carefully stepping out in her new high heeled sandals, Tabitha smiled her thanks and walked into the restaurant. The maître'd led her to one of the best tables in the house where Nik was already sitting with several other men, intently discussing something she didn't understand.

Nik had watched her walk across the restaurant and was furious. He noticed the red dress he'd chosen immediately but had had no idea what the silk would do to her figure. Before, she'd definitely had male attention, being lovely by herself. But now, in the red silk, clinging to every one of her soft, feminine curves, she was stunning and almost every male in the room had stopped to watch her walk, as well as many of the females who glared jealously at her spectacular figure.

He was sitting with several business associates, all of whom were trying to politely look at Nik but were unable to tear their attention from Tabitha and her new togs. Nik stood up abruptly and pulled out her chair, nodding to her before sitting down again. He continued the conversation, pulling everyone's attention back to him and not bothering to introduce her to the other gentlemen at the table. He simply wanted the meeting over and done with quickly so they would stop looking at her.

The meeting ended and Nik nodded, indicating that the other men should leave immediately, which they all understood and followed his unspoken command. When they were finally alone, Nik watched her as she fiddled nervously with her water glass.

"Quite the transformation," he said, taking a long swallow of his own ice water. His body wanted her immediately. He had no understanding of how she could tempt him with her lush body, but it was true. She wasn't the most beautiful woman he'd ever been with. But there was definitely an air about her, something that told the world that she was untouchable, unreachable. But he would touch her, he promised himself. Soon. In the meantime, he wanted to savor the power he currently had over her. He knew she'd had too much power over him for the past several years. Turning the tables was a heady experience.

"Why are you looking at me like that?" she asked, her voice breaking on her nervousness.

"You look lovely," he said. "All the other men in the restaurant are looking at you. Why not me as well?"

Tabitha blushed at his almost backhanded compliment, embarrassed by the hungry look in his eyes. "You're being silly," she said, shaking her head.

"Am I?" he countered. "Look around you."

Tabitha did and she noticed several men turn their heads away when she caught their stares. It scared her and she unconsciously moved closer to him, her body turning so she was almost protected by his arms. "Can we go?" she asked softly.

"Why would you want to do that?" he asked, somehow feeling mollified that she'd turned to him. He wasn't sure if she was even aware of it. She probably was, he told himself cynically. She knew all the tricks in the book and was a master at playing men to make them feel special. Lord knows she'd done that well enough during the first round. "You should bask in your glory, revel in the power you have over men and count your conquests."

"Stop it," she said nervously, dipping her head lower. "I don't like this. Could we please go? Or could I put on a sweater?" She crossed her arms self-consciously around herself, but knew she wasn't able to cover herself adequately. She'd felt so pretty in the dress only a few minutes earlier. But all the men's attentions had made her feel awkward, exposed.

"No. You need to eat something. I doubt you ate anything for breakfast and it is already two o'clock."

"I'm not really hungry," she argued, wanting only to get out of the stares of the people around her. "Couldn't we just leave?"

Nik sat forward and looked down into her eyes. "We can go back to my place."

"Fine," she said without thinking and stood up.

Nik followed her out, tossing some bills on the table to cover the lunch tab and tip. He glared at several men who were a little too obvious in their admiration for her. And even that action on his part bothered him. He had wanted this, wanted her to be objectified. Why was he now getting angry when other men thought it was okay to look her over like she was some sort of prize at an auction?

Back in the coolness of the limousine, he instructed his driver to take them back to his penthouse and then turned to face Tabitha.

"So what have you been doing for the past several years?" he asked conversationally.

Tabitha wasn't fooled. "Don't you already know?"

"No. I only know the bare facts. Tell me what you've been doing. What has occupied your time besides conquering the male population of the local villages?"

Tabitha wriggled uncomfortably. "I don't conquer males. In fact, I don't really have much to do with them at all."

"Despite all evidence to the contrary," he replied cynically.

"Isn't that the pot calling the kettle black? Not that I'm admitting to your accusation, though."

"It is curious that you would consider that an accusation. Perhaps you under sell yourself? No one willing to buy your charms for as high a price as your late husband?"

"Don't call him that!" she snapped.

That raised his eyebrows in surprise. "Testy," he replied. "Why?"

"Jerry Maxwell was nothing of what a husband should be."

"What, exactly, are your requirements for a perfect husband? I'd be very interested to hear them."

Tabitha was taken aback by the turn of the conversation but it was much better than some other possibilities. "I don't think I have a recipe for a perfect spouse, but I'm sure companionship would be at the top of the list."

"I'm guessing from your scathing tone, that you did not receive companionship from your late husband."

"I asked you not to call him that," she said angrily. "But no. Jerry and I didn't share much of anything."

"Except a home and a bed and a set of wedding rings. Minor things in your peculiar world, I suppose."

She closed her eyes briefly before opening them and staring out the window. "Don't assume anything, Nik." He couldn't know how painful this conversation was and she had no intention of letting him see how he was hurting her. She refused to give him any additional power. He had too much already.

He only smiled at her prickly response, making her feel strange and the butterflies started to flutter more frantically. "And your other requirements for a satisfying marriage?"

Tabitha huffed. "I don't know exactly what I'd like in a marriage. But I can guarantee that it wasn't received with Jerry."

"Pity," was all he said.

It only took a few minutes to reach an underground parking garage. He led her to a private elevator that immediately whisked them to the penthouse. There, Tabitha gasped in pleasure at the stunning view from his windows. "This is where you live?" she asked.

"When I'm in London," he said.

She turned away from the view to look at him, the smile of delight still on her face. "What do you mean?"

"I don't stay in one place very long. In fact, tomorrow we leave for Paris."

She was curious despite her need to stay aloof. "What will you be doing in Paris?"

Nik smiled but there was a sensual look to his eyes. "I have several meetings. You, on the other hand, will be enticing me away from those meetings, hopefully."

Tabitha blushed and turned away to stare out the window.

Thankfully, the phone rang at that moment and he picked up his cell phone. "Hello?" he answered, then started speaking in French, a language Tabitha only had a small amount of knowledge in so she was unable to follow the conversation.

She wandered over to a comfortable looking sitting area complete with a sofa and two overstuffed chairs surrounding a plasma screen television. With nothing else to do, she curled up on the sofa, tucking her feet underneath her and turned on the TV. After a sleepless night and all the tension of the day, she was exhausted. Within thirty minutes, she was asleep.

Tabitha didn't wake until the following morning. But she was no longer on the sofa. In fact, she was no longer dressed. Looking under the smooth, cotton sheets, she realized she was wearing only her red, lace underwear. Gasping, she looked around for Nik but didn't see him anywhere. She stilled and listened, but there were no sounds coming from anywhere in the penthouse.

Looking around, she started to see more of Nik's masculine personality coming out in the décor. The bedroom was enormous with beautiful, antique furnishings and a huge bed covered with a blue damask comforter. She felt like royalty as she looked around. Had she slept alone? No, she told herself, noticing the indentation on the pillow next to her. There was also a cell phone with a note. "Call me when you wake. N." was all it said.

Tabitha opened the phone and searched through the phone numbers. Sure enough, a number labeled "Nik" was already programmed into the memory. She pressed the number and held her breath, remembering the last time she had called Nik's cell phone and a woman had answered. If that was the case this time, she wasn't sure what she would do. But thankfully, his deep voice answered the phone with a simple, "Ne?"

"Nik?" she asked, not understanding anything of his native Greek language.

"Good morning," he said quickly. "I hope you are completely rested today."

"Yes. Thank you for asking."

"So polite!" he chuckled. "I'm asking since I wanted to warn you that I will not be so patient tonight. If you are tired, I will definitely wake you. Having you in my arms all night was too much of a temptation for any man to endure twice, Tabitha."

She cleared her throat and closed her eyes. "I understand."

There was a small, pregnant pause before he said, "Do you?"

"Yes," she said, nodding her head despite the fact that he couldn't see her. "You're telling me that our deal that started yesterday will be consummated tonight, regardless of my feelings or physical needs."

"On the contrary," he countered. "I will ensure that your physical needs are at the top of my list to satisfy," he said and laughed softly. "But you are correct in the fact that our deal will be consummated today. But in the meantime, a driver is waiting to take you to the airport. Wear something sexy." Without another word, the line was disconnected.

Tabitha stared at the phone angrily. She considered all her options but then thought of the villagers and all that they've gone through. It wasn't fair to them. She'd put them into this situation by not being more assertive. So basically, this was her penance. Shoving the sheets aside, she crawled out of bed and headed toward what she suspected was the bathroom. Showering helped her feel better and she tucked a towel around her and strolled to the closet. The first one was filled with men's clothes. The next contained the clothes Nik had chosen for her yesterday. She fingered through all the items, her mind whirling with the possibilities. She loved clothes but had never chosen things this risqué. But, if she only considered Nik's reaction, she couldn't deny how pretty and sexy she had felt walking into the restaurant yesterday, seeing the look of heat enter his eyes had been incredibly powerful. She liked that. She hadn't liked the other males' attention but they would be in more private places today she hoped.

Pulling out a suit, she considered her options. The jacket looked severe enough, she told herself. And if she wore the silk shirt underneath, with a lace bra….taking off the jacket at just the right time might give her a little more leverage. But did she have the courage? The silk was very delicate. He'd initially be angry that the outfit didn't fit his "sexy" definition. Smiling wickedly, she knew she was going to do it.

Drying her hair, she pulled it so the soft curls were piled on top of her head with only a few drifting down around her face. Pulling on the skirt, she realized that it wasn't as conservative as she'd originally thought. Hanging on the hanger, the soft black wool material looked like an ordinary straight skirt. But when she pulled it over her hips and zipped it up, she realized that it was made partly of a fabric that helped it stretch, so the fabric was tight around her hips. Searching through the drawers, she eventually found what she was looking for. Pulling off the regular lace underwear she'd originally chosen, she pulled on a tiny thong, then smoothed the black wool back down over her hips. Turning, she realized that it appeared that she was not wearing any underwear at all. Good!

She chose a demi cup bra that barely covered her nipples, then smoothed the luxurious silk over her shoulders. Smiling, she realized it had the exact effect she was hoping for. Put together, the suit was completely appropriate for the board room. But the lace bra showing discreetly through the silk was, in her mind, dangerously enticing.

She applied a light amount of makeup then stepped back to review her appearance in the full length mirror. Perfect! She looked like any business woman who might walk into the board room. But taking off her jacket, she turned into a sex kitten out to entice.

He wanted sexy! She'd give him sexy!

She pulled on a pair of stiletto shoes and walked out.

Nik's driver drove her directly to the airport with Jimmy, her body guard right behind her as she walked through the terminal. Apparently, this was a private plane so she was able to avoid security and the process was much easier and faster.

Boarding the plane, Tabitha ensured that her jacket was securely fastened before taking her seat in the jet. Nik boarded moments later with several men behind him. All of them were carrying large briefcase and looked very serious.

The plane was really a huge, flying office. There was a large conference area in the back where the men moved off to sit. The middle held smaller tables and chairs and the front was luxuriously appointed with a sofa, fully stocked bar and entertainment center.

As soon as Nik was seated, the plane took off. Within moments, they were leveling out and Nik started the conference with the men in the back. Tabitha picked up a magazine and ignored the entire situation although she nervously considered when she would take off her jacket. She would never have the nerve to do so in front of all those men. So she simply leaned back and read through article after article, bored when they continued to talk.

In Paris, they landed and Nik walked up to her. "I have meetings this afternoon. Here is some money," he said, handing her several large bills. "Go out and have a good time. Jimmy will take care of you. I'll meet you tonight," he said and disappeared down the stairs.

Tabitha was completely put out. Why on earth was she flying with him if all he was going to do was sit through meetings? Was it only a power thing? Of course it was! He wanted to know he could command her and order her about for pointless reasons.

Getting out of the plane, she walked down the stairs and ignored the men who were standing in the hot sunshine. She took off her jacket, irritated that she had even thought about trying to entice Nik. Feeling silly for her plan, she tossed her jacket in the back of the limousine, then ducked in herself.

Nik watched Tabitha disembark from the plane. He'd been distracted all morning, wondering what she was reading. He'd been hard pressed to pay attention to whatever the others were saying and so had extended the discussion, as if proving to himself that he was in control. He wouldn't go over to her no matter how lonely and bored she looked. She deserved it. She'd married herself off to a rich man and now she was a mistress to a rich man. Well this was what his life was like, he told himself.

Seeing the sun glint off her hair made his eyes stare. He actually had to grit his teeth as desire hit him hard. The skirt she was wearing wasn't as boring as he'd originally thought. The fabric clung to her hips and thighs, her derriere was nicely rounded and he had a perfect view of all her curves. But when she took off the jacket and he saw what she was wearing underneath, he almost punched the man speaking to him, irritated that someone would dare to interrupt that perfect moment as he viewed the sexy lace underneath the luxurious silk shirt.

Looking around after the car drove off, he was still feeling furious when he realized that others within the group had noticed, and they were still staring after the rapidly disappearing car.

Restraining himself from physical violence, he ducked into his own limousine and stared out the window, reviewing his plans for the day. He'd originally planned several meetings for the rest of the afternoon, then dinner with Tabitha and then to his Paris apartment. That would have to change now. He'd arrange for his cook to prepare dinner in house, he could cancel his last meeting and be back in only a few hours.

Calling Jimmy, he told him of his change in plans, noting with satisfaction that the man simply complied with his new agenda.

Glancing at his watch, Nik shifted uncomfortably in his seat. This was a new feeling, to be distracted by a woman. No, he corrected himself. He'd done it once before, four years ago. Nik had canceled and rearranged several meetings that week, calling into meetings instead of attending personally and having his helicopter fly him in and out of London constantly. Just to be around Tabitha. And then to realize that she was a fake and he the fool who had happily gone about dancing to her tune.

No more!

Five hours later, Nik stormed into his Paris penthouse, furious with himself for his inability to control the rampaging desire that had taken over his body earlier that morning, as well as the woman who had initiated that fury.

Not only had he adjusted his previously rigorous schedule after seeing Tabitha depart in the limousine earlier that day. He had also canceled several other meetings then phoned Jimmy to ensure that she was back where he could vent his anger at her.

But as he stood in the white marble foyer, his steps faltered and eventually came to a complete halt. Standing against the vivid backdrop of the city of Paris in springtime, was the woman who had occupied his thoughts almost constantly for the past several weeks, stirring his body to a state of arousal on so many occasions and generally at the most inopportune moments. He watched in amazement and almost mind-boggling suspense as she reached her slender arms up and pulled the pins from her softly curling hair, allowing the unencumbered masses to waft gently down against her delicate shoulders. He couldn't see her face, but the outline of her body, her curves, lit the fire that had been smoldering all afternoon.

Walking forward, he was almost transfixed by the sight of her as she rubbed her shoulders, lifted her hair up and gently kneaded her neck muscles as if she had been concentrating on issues of great import all afternoon but had finally realized that it was time to relax and delve into the evening and mindlessness. Nik agreed. It was definitely time to stop thinking. All he wanted was to pull her into his arms, kiss her pouty mouth and imprint himself onto her consciousness so she could think of no other man.

Reaching her, his steps slowed as he allowed the soft, feminine scent of her to waft into his nostrils. It wasn't perfume he smelled, but something much more subtle, more unidentifiable and therefore, much more alluring. His hand slowly slid up her spine and he smiled as she jumped and spun around.

"Nik!" she gasped, dropping her hands to her sides and taking a step back. "I didn't know you'd come in," she said, looking around. When she saw no one else in the penthouse with them, her anxiety ridden eyes snapped back to his darker, more mysterious gaze. "Where's Jimmy?" she asked nervously, worried about what would happen next.

"Gone," he said simply and took her hands in his, lacing her fingers with his own and pulling her gently forward.

"Why on earth would you send him away?" she asked nervously, resisting the pull of his hands. But Nik was relentless. "He was going to check the kitchen for the other staff."

Nik brought her forward several inches, then dropped her fingers, wrapping his arms around her waist as a more efficient method of getting her where he wanted her to be, touching him from knee to shoulder. "He was no longer needed," Nik replied in answer to her question.

"But I was hungry," she countered warily. She wasn't, at least not anymore. She was terrified and that fear eclipsed whatever minor hunger pains had been gnawing at her a moment ago.

"I'll make sure you're every need is fulfilled," he said a moment before his mouth captured hers. He felt her lips tremble initially and slowed down, not wanting their first time together to be rushed. This woman had been the star of so many fantasies over the past several years, he wanted to make sure each of them were realized.

His lips caressed, nibbled enticed and teased until he felt her relax slightly. Then he pulled her closer, his other arm wrapping around her shoulders to press her soft breasts against his chest. He imagined he could feel the lace of her bra through the silk of her shirt but knew that was impossible. He was still wearing his business suit for starters. But he'd thought about that bra for so many hours, remembered the red lace she'd worn the night before as she'd wrapped her arms around his waist, holding onto him as if she had been afraid he would leave. So finally having her exactly where he wanted her, and awake, he could be excused for imagining something that was probably impossible. He would feel it and see it soon enough. And he'd feel that lace not through his shirt and hers, but against his skin and under his fingertips.

Pulling the silk shirt free from the waistband of her skirt, his fingers skimmed lightly across her satin skin, enjoying the soft gasp that came from her throat. Deepening the kiss, he pushed his tongue into her mouth, caressing her tongue, enticing her to mimic his movements. She was the perfect student and, just as she had so many years ago, she knew exactly how to react to him, muttering soft moans and gasps, whimpering when his hand moved higher.

Her arms finally reached up and wrapped around his neck, pulling him closer, just as he remembered her doing during their first kiss. Her back arched as his hand went higher. He was tempted to release the clasp to her bra, freeing her full, perfect breasts for his touch, but his mind was clamoring for a sight of her body in the lace. The lace that he'd bought. She was all his, every inch of her and everything that covered her, he'd provided. The thought was heady and only intensified the heat scorching his body.

Nik released the closure of her skirt, allowing the fabric to skim down her hips and pool at her feet. When his hands ventured lower, he almost lost the control he'd been fighting for all day when his palm touched bare skin. The tiny string crossing her back made him haul her closer, higher against his aching need. Giving in to the desire, he swung her up into his arms and carried her into the bedroom.

Standing next to the bed, he lowered her slowly to the floor, his mouth covering hers again, pulling her body close, then stepping away and pulling the silk blouse off her. He stood, staring at her in the creamy lace bra and thong underwear, her feet still in the stiletto heels and his mind simply stopped functioning.

"You're more beautiful than I ever imagined," he said, his voice hoarse.

Tabitha stood in front of Nik, her mind had turned to mush about fifteen minutes ago, about the same time his strong, lean fingers touched her skin. When he only stood in front of her, his business jacket still on, something inside her snapped. She could no longer take the torment from him and moved forward, pushing the perfectly tailored material off his broad shoulders. His tie came off just as quickly but she had no idea where it landed and her fingers trembled with need and urgency as they worked the buttons on his shirt. When his chest was finally bared to her hungry gaze, she reached up and tentatively touched his chest. The scattering of hair was mesmerizing, as were the muscles underneath. She hadn't bothered to push it off, but when the fabric got in her way, she ripped further, her curious mind demanding to know all.

She heard a groan but paid little attention to it until his hands reached up and clasped her own. She felt the soft mattress beneath her shoulders and her eyes implored him to follow. But he stopped and Tabitha was able to watch in fascination as he pulled off his pants, standing in front of her in only his boxers. A moment later, he was completely, uninhibitedly naked in front of her and the full extent of his manhood stood proudly at the juncture of his hips. He was incredible, like nothing she'd ever imagined before.

Looking up, she caught his gaze which then pinned her to the bed. "I want you," he said roughly and came down on top of her, his arms holding his weight as his mouth came down to cover her nipple, tasting, teasing, nipping gently at the center before licking to sooth the ache. Tabitha cried out, her hands gripping his shoulders as the tidal wave of desire tore through her body, flooding her senses so she was aching with a need she didn't understand. Her fingers sliced into his hair, both holding his head to her breast, yet also needing to pull him away, to stop the fire that was building to a painful intensity she didn't understand. When he finally pulled away, his head moved, but only so his mouth could cover the other nipple. Her hips rocked, her back arched but nothing would relieve the ache in her stomach, in every cell of her body.

When his hand moved downwards, she grabbed his wrist, her head shaking in fear. "No, please!" she pleaded with him. "I don't understand," she said, unable to even voice her confusion.

"Yes," he rasped, grabbing her hands with his other, holding both of hers up over her head as his hand moved down, exploring her skin, grazing along her outer thighs, then moving insistently up the insides. Her thighs opened, somehow understanding what her mind couldn't comprehend and his mouth smiled in appreciation for her body's reception. His fingers moved slowly, relentlessly upwards, teasing and fluttering until she groaned and closed her eyes.

When his fingers moved inside her, she arched again, instinctively moving against his fingers and her body, so new to these startling sensations, climaxed almost instantly. Her eyes squeezed shut as her body convulsed, then slowly floated back down to earth.

But there was no escape. Nik would not allow her to stop. As soon as her body slowed, his mouth returned to her breast, teasing her right back to the frantic state she had been in only moments before. His mouth moved from her breast to her stomach, his tongue and teeth exploring her body, tasting and finding new ways to increase the tension to a higher level than before.

A tear escaped her eyes and she wanted to fight him, needing him but not wanting the almost painful pleasure his hands were delivering with each, unerring touch to her skin.

"Nik!" she cried out. "Please no more," she begged. "I can't take it anymore!"

He was gone for only a moment, returning to place the condom on his erection. Then he pulled her hands back over her head and pushed himself gently between her thighs. "Look at me, Tabitha," he demanded, his body moving against hers, eliciting yet another gasp of pleasure before she complied with his order.

As she opened her eyes to watch, she noticed the perspiration on his forehead and the glistening on his shoulders. Wrapping her legs around his hips, she begged with her eyes, pleading with him to end the torture. With one, strong urgent thrust, he pushed himself into her heat. Instantly, the pain tore through her and she cringed, pulling back to avoid the pain again.

Nik froze, his eyes looking into hers and revealing the shock his invasion caused. "Tabitha?" he groaned, his body unable to move, just as the pleasure of her tight sheath clasped him even more into her core. "Look at me," he said as softly as he could under the circumstances.

She shook her head and bit her lower lip. "Please. Are we done yet?" she asked, the strain of keeping still almost too much for her. She wanted to move and every cell in her body was begging for release, but she didn't want to move for fear that the pain would return. "Is it over?" she asked when he didn't say anything.

"No," he groaned. "I'm sorry. How...?" he started to ask, only to have her hand cover his mouth.

"I'm sorry, Nik. I'm sure you have many questions but couldn't you just...." She searched for the right words but nothing came to mind. It was difficult to be eloquent at the moment. "finish?" she said lamely.

Nik put his head down onto her shoulder for a long moment, his breathing coming hard and his body aching for release. But he stopped himself and looked back up at her. "If I'd known..." he started to say.

"But you didn't," she interrupted.

"No. I didn't," he said. "But I can make it better," he promised. With a gentle movement, he showed her. And Tabitha's eyes widened when there was no pain. When he moved again, she actually felt good. By the time he pulled almost all the way out, then gently moved back again, her body was back in the throes of desire, the need for release just as demanding as it had been before the invasion.

Nik used every ounce of his control to slow the pace. But her body moving against his felt too good and after several minutes, he could no longer hold back. Reaching down between their bodies, he helped her come to a climax that had her crying out and holding his shoulders, her nails digging into his skin. A few minutes later, he too came in a climax that seemed to stop his heartbeat for several long minutes. Their breathing sounded ragged, desperate as they both stared into each other's eyes, their bodies throbbing with the culmination of four years of wanting.

Tabitha lay in the center of his strong, muscular arms, his head against her shoulder and the two of them intimately connected. As reality slowly returned, she smiled, understanding dawning on her at last. So this was sex? Interesting. No, fascinating, she told herself.

As he rolled onto his back, pulling her with him so she was draped across his chest, she marveled at the amazing feelings her body had experienced. She wanted to laugh out loud, but wasn't sure what the protocol was for this kind of thing.

Nik looked up at her and she turned her face away, looking out the window, afraid he would ask questions or say something mean that would change this whole experience for her.

"Tabitha, did I mistake what just happened?" he asked.

Tabitha turned her head back and noticed he was staring at the ceiling.

"I think we both had sex," she said and pulled out of his arms. Sitting up, she was immediately self-conscious of her nakedness so she pulled the blanket from the bottom of the bed and wrapped it around herself, standing up and moving toward the bathroom.

"Tabitha!" he called out to her, but she ignored him and continued on her search for a shower. She opened one door and discovered it filled with clothes. The next door, thankfully, was the bathroom.

The bathroom was done in black marble and all the fixtures were ultra-modern and shining with pristine newness. Turning on the shower, she shivered, afraid he would follow her and wondering how she was going to get out of the conversation. She didn't want anyone to know about her horrible marriage. It was too humiliating.

She had just turned on the shower when Nik walked in behind her. Pulling her back against his chest, he looked at her in the mirror. "You know I'm going to get the answers one way or another, Tabitha. Don't you?"

She shivered and shook her head. "No. That's my own business. It has nothing to do with the situation we're currently in," she said and pulled out of his arms.

He allowed her to go but stood watching her as she dropped the blanket before stepping into the shower. The warm spray smoothed her hair down against her back creating a slick look to the tresses that fascinated him. Gone were the thoughts about her marriage and her virginity. Gone also were the gentlemanly thoughts and guilt that had surged through him when he realized that she was untutored in the ways of sex. All that consumed him was this driving need to possess her again.

In the past, women had interested him and some could even entice him sexually to a certain point. But only to a point and only if it was convenient to him. Normally, he called the shots as well as when and where. But Tabitha was different and for the life of him, he couldn't figure out how to work her out of his system. He wanted her again which wasn't abnormal since he had a driving sexual appetite. But this need for her was beyond what he was used to and comfortable with.

Stepping into the shower, he took the soap from her hands and lathered her soft, silken skin. He shampooed her hair all the while trying to maintain a cool distance from her. But the soft sighs that came from her as he massaged her scalp and back were driving him crazy. He had been hard when he'd watched her walk across the room but now, he could no longer wait. He had to have her. Lifting her up, he pushed her gently against the marble wall of the shower, rinsing her off as he took a nipple into his mouth. He knew he should give her some time to recover, that she might be in pain. But he didn't care. He had to have her again. He promised himself he would be extra gentle this time. He quickly donned protection with one hand while he held her against him with his other arm.

Pushing into her, he slowed his pace enough to watch her reactions, noting with agonizing satisfaction that her eyes were closed tightly and her mouth was open, as if the pleasure were too much for her. He knew how she felt. Feeling himself slide inside her, watching her reactions was pushing him to the edge. He forced himself to slow. But when he felt her start to convulse around him, he released his control and drove himself into her soft, yielding flesh, climaxing for a second time in less than a half hour.

They stayed like that for a long time, the warm water pulsing down on their skin as the reality of the situation came back to them. He'd never been so impatient to have made love in the shower, and against the wall. But looking down into her smiling face, he knew he'd definitely do this again.

"Are you okay?" he asked, gently pushing her wet hair out of her face.

"Yes," she sighed, her arms limp around his shoulders. "Definitely yes," she said and laid her head against his chest.

Nik chuckled deeply and pulled her closer, hugging her slim body that seemed to fit against him as if she were made for him. "I'd better get you out of here," he said and turned off the water. He wrapped her into a large, fluffy white towel before pulling one around his waist. "What did you do today?"

he asked, startled that he genuinely wanted to hear how she'd spent her afternoon.

"Oh, Nik!" she enthused, pulling the towel around her and tucking the corner under her arm. "I went to see Notre Dame and it was beautiful. I was going to see the Eifel Tower but then Jimmy got a phone call and he rushed me back here. But still, it was thrilling to see things I'd only heard about before."

Nik looked down at her in confusion. "Your father was not poor. Why didn't he ever take you to Paris before?"

Tabitha shrugged as she pulled a comb through her hair. "My father didn't like traveling. I went to boarding school for high school and finishing school but even that was only to Northern England and he didn't come with me to drop me off. He simply handed me a train ticket and told me to get there on time."

Nik didn't like her father, remembering the one conversation he'd had with him. But it still seemed odd that the man was so heartless to his daughter. "What was he like?" Nik asked against his better judgment.

Tabitha's smile disappeared and she put down the comb before walking away. "He was a good man," was all she would say. How did one describe a father who had sold her to a man who had no interest in her simply to save his failing business? But was she any better? The idea stopped her in the middle of the bedroom. She really wasn't any better, she realized. She was selling herself to Nik just to save the business. Well, not really the business but all the people who supported the business, she corrected. She didn't want the town to die and so here she was. But was this really so bad? She was living a life more luxurious than she'd ever imagined she could live, she was with the man she'd fallen in love with several years ago and this time, the affair might last a little longer than the week she'd had before.

Shouldn't she be excited for this opportunity? She looked back at Nik who was walking out of the bathroom. He looked at her curiously, one dark eyebrow raised in question. Biting her lower lip, she considered the idea that had occurred to her. Could she do it? Could she use Nik the way her mind was asking her to use him?

It had been so long since she'd felt like a woman and the way Nik liked her to dress, to walk and definitely the way he looked at her made her feel wanted and beautiful.

He was using her for his revenge purposes. What was the difference? All she wanted was to feel pretty and sexy and maybe wanted sexually. After her horrific marriage, was that so wrong? And maybe she could learn to entice a man, show him that she was a real woman. And perhaps she could prove it to herself in the process.

She watched as Nik pulled on a pair of well-worn jeans. If she was going to learn anything, she couldn't ask for a better teacher. Even now after her body had been satisfied twice with amazing results, watching him walk and comb his hair, she wanted him again. She could feel her body react, her nipples harden and that secret place between her legs become liquid all over again. Turning away so he couldn't see her face, she knew she was blushing with all the ideas that were singing through her brain.

Why not? She was caught in this situation. He was probably more than willing to teach her anything she wanted to know. What would be the problem if he didn't know he was teaching her?

"Are you hungry?" Nik asked from close behind her.

Tabitha startled, swinging around as if she'd been caught doing something naughty. Which, if he could read her mind, he'd know she was. "Excuse me?"

Nik's eyes looked down into her blue ones and knew she was hiding something. The soft flush that stole across her cheeks confirmed it. "What are you thinking about?" he demanded, catching her upper arm and turning her back to face him.

"Nothing," she said and looked straight ahead at his chest. Not a good idea with her current plans still formulating in her mind. She looked out the window, assuming that was a safer idea.

"I don't think it was nothing. But you're probably not going to tell me, are you?" he asked, trying to keep the anger from his tone. The woman was going to drive him crazy with her little mysteries. Was she thinking about the other men she'd had in her life? Was she comparing him to them? No, that's not possible, he thought to himself. She hadn't experienced them sexually. So what had she been thinking, dammit! He wished he could just walk away but she was slowly becoming an obsession he had to have.

Tabitha smiled up at him, her eyes bright and cheerful and definitely wicked. "No. I'm not going to tell you," she laughed, delighted with her plans and deciding to go ahead with them. She licked her lips and shook her head again. "But I can tell you that I'm famished," she started only to see the smile

61

creep into his eyes…"for food!" she laughed, then wondered why she'd stopped his mind from traveling down the path she was already on. Her body wanted him, why would she stop another lesson?

She felt her cheeks heating once again and quickly spoke to distract him. "And you promised to satisfy all of my physical needs. So what are you going to feed me?"

Sighing, Nik rolled his eyes, satisfied slightly now that she was looking at him instead of seeming to be thinking of someone else. "Fine. Get some clothes on and meet me in the dining room. I'll see what the cook has made for dinner," he said and left the bedroom barefoot and bare chested.

Chapter 5

Tabitha looked across the palazzo and smiled, enjoying the heat of the early afternoon and the rush of people buzzing around busily. Florence was definitely a beautiful city, she thought as she felt the sun heat her face. She had her book on her lap and was staring into space, not really caring about anything around her.

She and Nik had left Paris yesterday to arrive here in Florence last night. She hadn't seen him much today and didn't expect to see him until the evening. He'd told her to dress up tonight but she had no idea what that meant.

Jimmy was sitting at the next table pretending to not be there, and she was slowly learning to ignore his presence, although he was such a bulky man, it was hard to do at times. When they were in the limousine together, he sat in the front seat, usually with the privacy screen closed. When they walked, he maintained a few feet between the two of them, never getting close unless he was opening a door or if the street traffic was unusually heavy. It was as if the man were deliberately keeping a distance from her. She'd come to accept it but at times it still bothered her. She felt like a nuisance.

On the other hand, she loved the fact that she had a car waiting for her convenience and Nik had handed her a wallet this morning filled with credit cards and cash. She didn't like that too much, feeling cheap and awkward. But it was certainly nice to relax and enjoy sightseeing. She'd had no idea how much she liked to travel, not understanding her father's insistence that it was too much trouble. Although traveling with Nik was a completely different experience. When he walked somewhere, no matter what city they were in, it was like Moses parting the red sea. People seemed to naturally move out of his way for him. There was always a car, helicopter, plane or other transportation available and waiting on his convenience. So perhaps normal travel would be annoying. But she certainly liked this.

She also liked looking over at Nik and finding him staring back at her. On the plane, she'd heard his voice and just knew that he was looking at her. Sure enough, when she'd raised her head from the magazine to look around, his eyes were on her, his thumb rubbing along his jaw and she just knew that he was thinking about having sex with her. The flush that had stolen through her body at that moment had caused a chuckle to come from him and she shifted uncomfortably in her leather chair, unable to maintain his gaze.

The conversations around the palazzo now were mostly in Italian, so when she heard English, she was surprised and looked up, hiding her confusion behind the large cup of cappuccino she had ordered.

The two men were tossing out ideas on how to resolve a problem and Tabitha's stomach clenched, realizing that MacComber Industries could help these men out at a lower cost than the numbers they were currently discussing.

Could it really be that simple? Tabitha was too excited for a moment, but when the men started to pull their papers together, as if they were finished with their brainstorming, Tabitha decided it was better to be rude and wrong than to lose the opportunity.

"Excuse me," she said, standing up herself. The two men looked down at her, initially surprised. But then both smiled as they looked down at her petite form. "I'm sorry to have eavesdropped on your conversation, but you might want to consider another idea. It is cheaper and probably more efficient than what you were discussing," she said and the three of them sat down and she took out a paper to write some notes.

The men were eager for more information and Tabitha, who had never been allowed in any meetings before her father's death, was surprised at how much she actually knew about the factory and its operations. The two men were considering a large issue and it would mean a big contract for MacComber if they decided to go with her idea. Even if they didn't go through with the contract, it was still thrilling to know that she could actually discuss the details of a project with potential clients intelligently.

When the men left, Tabitha could only sit at the table, smiling like a silly little school girl who had just been kissed by her first boyfriend. To complicate the issue, her first thought was to tell Nik. But would he even care? This could boost profits and revenue significantly, but Nik's whole purpose in buying the company was revenge on her.

Pushing that thought aside, she decided to revel in her success and hold it close. Talking to Nik would only crush her happiness, despite the fact that she desperately wanted to talk with him. If he showed even the slightest indifference, it would diminish this wonderful feeling she had right now.

Instead, she smiled to Jimmy, who nodded in response, and decided to walk through the beautiful city, touring the sites. For lunch, she bought some fruit at a roadside stand and continued walking, eager to see as much of the city as possible before she was called back by Nik. By the middle of the afternoon, she was staring up at the Cathedral of Santa Maria del Fiore, marveling at the beauty of the architecture and art. The marble and chrome was astonishing and the enormous size of the building and Piazza was a tribute to Brunelleschi's faith.

When the thought struck her that she wished she could tour this fabulous city with Nik, she was concerned. Why on earth did she have the desire to share things with Nik? He was wonderfully generous with her, handing her a wallet filled with cash and credit cards and a closet full of clothes that she'd never find the time to wear in a year. But this was beyond material things. She wanted to experience things with him and get excited next to him as they viewed this city.

Biting her lip in confusion, Tabitha moved through the cathedral, impressed with the works of art but concerned about her feelings for a man she'd known for a total of ten days out of her entire life. The first five days had been blissful, but he had broken her heart and was now treating her like his mistress, or worse. Why didn't that bother her? Was she willing to excuse his behavior simply because he made her feel things in bed that she'd never felt, never wanted to feel, with another man?

Tabitha moved along, heading toward the Academia Gallery. She stood in line for three hours but eventually, she was able to see the magnificent "David". Stunned by the famous statue, her thoughts again turned to Nik.

Back out on the street, she turned to Jimmy and sighed. "Any idea what is on the agenda for the rest of the day?" she asked.

Jimmy took out his cell phone and pressed a few buttons. "I believe Kirios Andretti will be attending the opera tonight. Would you like to return to the palazzo to prepare?"

Tabitha considered the time. It was already three o'clock in the afternoon. "I guess that would be fine," she said, wishing she didn't have to go to the opera. She disliked that form of theatre, thinking that the actors were just screaming. She could barely understand the words even if the songs were in English, which they rarely were. "What time is Nik expected back?" she asked.

"Not for several hours," he replied, his dark eyes not revealing any emotion or reaction.

"Okay. I guess I'd better start to get ready. I need to get my nails done, don't I?" she asked, looking down at her nail polish that was now chipped in several places since she hadn't received a manicure in three days. With her thin nails, she needed to go without nail polish, which is what she'd done before Nik arrived in her life, or she needed to get a manicure every day.

Tabitha allowed herself to be driven back to Nik's palazzo but she didn't really feel like dressing for the night. She wanted to savor her day, hug it close to her and think about the possibilities.

Unfortunately, Nik had already returned when she walked in. "Where the hell have you been?" he demanded when he first caught sight of her.

Instantly on the defensive, Tabitha calmly put her purse down on a glass topped table and inhaled deeply, trying to not react to his anger. "I have been out touring the sites," she explained, crossing her arms over her chest.

"Who with?"

Tabitha didn't like the way this conversation was heading. "Jimmy," was all she said initially. Then with the doubtful look in his eyes, she asked, "Who did you think I was out with?"

"I saw you at the Piazza today. You were sitting at a table with two men. It looked rather cozy. Explain that to me!"

Tabitha drew herself up to her full height, uncaring that he still towered over her by more than a foot. "No. I'm not explaining anything to you!" she yelled at him, angry now that she was being accused of something ridiculous. "How in the world did you know where I was anyway?"

"I always know where you are. Jimmy is right behind you at all times and I called him to surprise you for lunch. Obviously, I was the one surprised," he said, his voice not yelling but coldly angry.

"Well it is none of your business, but I wasn't having lunch with the men. If you'd bothered to come along and talk to me, let me know you were there and not lurking around like some lizard about to jump on its prey, then you would have heard my conversation."

"What were you talking about?" he demanded, moving closer to her so he was towering above her.

Tabitha was determined not to be intimidated. "I'm not going to tell you! Since you already think the worst of me, which you have absolutely no right to do, then I'll just let you think it. There's nothing I can tell you that you don't already know about me, is there? Since you have me all figured out already, just make up the conversation I'd had and go with that. The truth has never bothered you from making accusations before. Don't let it hinder your horrible opinion of me now!"

Without another word, she spun on her heel and walked out of the beautiful salon. And to think, the obnoxious man had been on her mind all day, wishing that he'd been there with her to see the things she was seeing and share the excitement of her first potential business sale. "Arrr!" she said, slamming the door to the bedroom where her clothes had apparently been stored.

She stomped around the room, considering her options and coming up with none. She couldn't leave, afraid that he'd follow through on his threat to sell off the company. She couldn't move into a different room because she had no idea where they were. This bedroom took over more than half of this end of the hallway.

When he walked into the room behind her and closed the door, she glared at him. Moving off to the closet where she'd been shown her clothes earlier that day, she searched for some idea. When her eyes caught on a swimsuit, she pulled it down angrily. Stripping out of her clothes, she pulled it on, uncaring of the color or the style, just so long as she had some way of getting away from the man.

She walked out of the closet, noticing that he had taken off his jacket and tie, strolling closer to the bed but was still glaring at the door to her closet where she'd disappeared. She pulled her eyes away from him and buried her fascination with the man's body. She told herself she would not care that he might be about to get undressed.

"I'm going for a swim," she called out only moments before walking out of the bedroom.

It took her fifteen minutes of searching, and even then she had to ask a passing servant, but eventually she found out where the pool was. Diving into the crystal water of the indoor pool, she tried to release the anger that was pulsing through her. How dare he accuse her of cheating on him! What right did he have to make that kind of assumption anyway? And why had he told her that he'd be busy all day, only to show up and want to have lunch with her? That idea thawed some of her anger, but she was still resentful that he hadn't just come up to her and asked her what was going on.

"What the…?" Tabitha gasped as she felt something swish by her leg. A second later, her waist was seized by two strong hands. Tossed over Nik's shoulder, she screamed out in fear. "What are you doing?" she demanded as her wet hair flopped over her face, blocking out her vision until she angrily swiped it away.

Nik pulled her off his shoulder so she was cradled in his arms. His angry expression was staring straight ahead as he walked over to one of the large lounge chairs.

"Nik! What are you doing! I'm not going to…" whatever she'd been about to say was knocked out of her as his lips covered her mouth, his hands quickly taking off her bathing suit. Standing naked in the pool area, wet and suddenly hot for his hands, his touch, was a deliciously naughty feeling.

"We can't do this here!" she said, trying to pull out of his arms. "What do you think you're doing?"

"Shut up," he growled a moment before his mouth latched onto her nipple.

Inhaling sharply, Tabitha's head lolled back on her neck, her back arched and her mind emptied of everything. "What are you doing?" she asked, but then her mind blanked again as his fingers slid down her rib cage erotically.

He didn't answer her. Instead, he lowered her to the large chaise lounge and finished pulling off her wet bathing suit. He then stripped himself of his and covered her naked body with his own.

Tabitha had never known that such all-consuming and immediate passion could swell up within her. But when he slid his hands down her body, his fingers slowly entering her and driving her mad with wanting, she was mindless and desperate for release.

Nik had tried to hold off. Watching her leave the bedroom several minutes ago, he had been angrier than he'd ever been in his life. Upon examination, he realized that it was jealously. Plain and simple jealousy and he didn't like that feeling at all, never having experienced it before. Prior to meeting Tabitha, if a woman was interested and he was interested, then all was good. When the mood ran out for either party, then the liaison was over and both could go their separate ways. Nik knew that it was usually him who pulled out of the relationship before the women, but he'd never promised more than a good time. If the woman was disappointed that her hopes of something more were unfulfilled, he had no responsibility on that front.

But with Tabitha, everything was different. When she'd stormed out of the bedroom, he'd been furious. First of all, he'd never had a woman push his buttons like she could. And no one, positively no one, walked out on him. Financially, he would destroy a man, or woman, for that matter, if they'd even tried to leave before he was done with the conversation. But Tabitha didn't seem to know or care about the power he held over her. And when she'd left, underneath the anger and jealousy, was actual respect; yet another feeling he'd never had for a woman.

Following her into the pool, he'd been determined to finish the argument and make her bend to his will. He would never allow her to see another man while he was still interested. The fury he'd let fester all afternoon had exploded the moment he'd seen her walk through the front door of his house. But when he'd walked into the pool area, he'd been struck by a powerful desire to possess her, to make her writhe under him and fill her with thoughts of nothing but him. When he'd pulled her into his arms, his intention had been to make love to her slowly so she was begging him, pleading with him to give her release.

Now staring down at her slender, beautiful body, he was actually her slave. He wanted to fill her up and give her the satisfaction she was demanding. How could she just move slightly and he was mindless? It was unheard of!

But as he slowly filled her, he stared down into her sexy, sultry eyes and his muscles were shaking with his need to move slower, control the pace. Unfortunately, with one single movement from her, he was unable to stop. Filling her up, moving inside her, watching her facial expressions and knowing the moment when she was about to find her release made him feel strong and powerful itself. Lifting her higher, adjusting his movements slightly, he helped her over the edge to her climax. And when he heard her small cries of release, it was all the help he needed to find his own release. Just as it always was with this tiny woman, when it came, it was powerful, all consuming and mind-blowing.

Breathing heavily, he pulled her onto his chest, his hands running through her wet hair as he enjoyed hearing her small gasps and sighs as she slowly came down from the high of their lovemaking. It was actually better than it had been the first time, he thought to himself. Smiling, he considered that, although he hadn't gone slowly, he'd still accomplished his goal of making her realize that she was his and no one would get near her.

"We need to get ready for the opera," he said, his voice thick and hoarse.

Tabitha sighed heavily and turned her head so her chin was resting on his chest. "Do we have to?" she asked, her eyes starting to close.

Nik laughed and sat up, bringing her with him so she was now sitting on his lap. She started to reach for her bathing suit to pull it back on but he simply stood up, effectively putting the garment out of her reach. "Yes. We have to." He carried her over to the pool and started down the steps.

"Nik, stop this right now!' she said, glancing back over her shoulder to the bathing suit on the floor. "I have to put on my suit. I can't go in here like this," she gasped.

"Why not?" he laughed at her outraged expression.

"Because it is indecent," she said, her arms holding him around his shoulders.

"So?" he shrugged. "It's my house. My pool and I want to swim in it naked. Who is going to stop me?" he asked, pulling her down into the water and taking her hands as he swam backwards.

Tabitha's eyes closed slightly as she felt him underneath her. Feeling the water swish over her naked body, and his dark skin so close to hers, but not touching was an extremely sensuous feeling. She couldn't believe that she was already aching for him again with so little time between the last satisfying encounter with him. Clenching her teeth, she tried to ignore the gentle friction their bodies were creating. But when her stomach realized that he was just as affected, her eyes flew open, noticing that he was looking down at her, his eyes blaring his desire.

Without a word, he pulled her up against his chest. The second time, with the water splashing around them, creating additional friction was too much and Tabitha took control, needing to find the release. She grabbed his shoulders, her legs wrapped around his waist and she set the pace and the angle, biting her lower lip and closing her eyes as she climaxed around his hard length and thrilling when she pulled him along moments after, feeling powerful and amazingly sexy.

Chapter 6

Tabitha looked around and took a sip of champagne. It was icy cool and felt good along her throat. Unfortunately, it wasn't her throat she needed to cool down. Nik had his arm around her waist and her mind was remembering the episode in the pool earlier in the afternoon. Nik had smiled down at her, as if he was proud of her aggressive behavior but she was embarrassed that she'd taken control like that. Although it had been a very heady experience.

"People are going to start wondering if you have a fever, my dear," he said against her ear, his deep voice chuckling and his mouth biting her ear lobe gently.

"Stop it," she said, knowing that her cheeks were turning a darker shade of red.

Her words only increased Nik's amusement. "Sorry but I don't think I can. You look absolutely stunning with that sweet blush on your cheeks. It keeps reminding me of the moment you realized what you'd done."

"Nik! Forget this afternoon," she demanded and tried to turn away from him. But he was having none of that and pulled her back against his side, laughing out right now.

At that moment, a business acquaintance came up and greeted Nik who immediately introduced her to him. He was a very nice man and his wife arrived a moment later. They laughed and discussed previous events that had brought them together as well as previous places they had been separately. Tabitha should have felt left out, since she hadn't been part of the guest list they were discussing nor any of the places they had been but Nik smiled down into her eyes and explained the inside joke to her make her feel included and accepted. Despite her admonitions against the feelings, Tabitha felt a deep connection at that moment with Nik. And something slightly more that she wasn't going to define. Thankfully, the lights dimmed, bells chimed

71

subtly and Nik excused himself from his friends, guiding her back to his private box in the opera house.

As they took their seats again, Tabitha considered the man at her side. He was incredibly handsome, that was a given. But he was also amazingly intelligent. She remembered his conversations on the plane yesterday as well as the day before. Not only was he insightful but also had a staggering ability to retain and recall facts and figures. While the rest of the people around the conference table had been scrambling through their papers, Nik stated the figures from memory. It was a testament to how easily his brain could consider all aspects of a business deal and come out with the most profitable solution.

People seemed to flock to him too. Nik had no patience for pointless conversation, but over and over again in social settings, she'd seen people walk up and ask him his opinion on varied matters. Nik always had an answer and was more than willing to talk.

Struggling to come to terms with his anger earlier, she considered the scene he might have come upon earlier in the day. She had been so eager to discuss what MacComber Industries could do for the men's business problem, she might have appeared to be interested in them as men as well. That hadn't been the case, and she had in fact been thinking about Nik the whole time and wondering if he might have said something better to convince them to use the factory, wishing he were there to help her. But she could now see how it might have appeared to him if he had come upon the scene suddenly.

After the opera, they joined a group of people at a restaurant for dinner. The meal was delicious, with five courses and wines that seemed to flow freely. But all Tabitha wanted to do was to get Nik alone so she could apologize and explain what had happened. She knew she should have done it earlier in the day, when he'd first brought it up to her, but she'd been so taken aback by his anger, she'd only seen red herself.

"What's wrong?" Nik demanded as soon as Jimmy closed the limousine door behind them. "You've been extremely quiet all through dinner and I don't think you paid attention to the opera after the intermission, although I would have sworn you were enjoying it earlier. What happened? Did someone say something to you to hurt your feelings?" he asked, his eyes watching her features closely.

Tabitha smiled gently up at his handsome, concerned face. "No. I just thought about what you might have seen earlier in the Piazza and wanted to explain. I apologize if you misunderstood my talking with those two men earlier. I promise, it wasn't what you think."

Taking a deep breath, she noticed that his eyes had hardened and she could see that he was closing off to her. Speaking quickly, she reached up and took his hand. "The men were talking about how their current factory was making mistakes over and over again, diminishing their profit margins. The factory was outdated apparently and the owner wasn't willing to work with them to increase their productivity."

"You should have mentioned MacComber. From what I've read on the reports, they can re-tool quickly to get more out of the assembly lines," Nik said stiffly.

Tabitha grinned. "That's exactly what I did." Turning to face him, she unconsciously pulled his hand against her stomach in her excitement and her eyes and face became more animated. "Oh, Nik! It was so exciting to know that my company…well" she faltered, "your company now technically, could not only solve their problems, but also that I knew so much about the systems and the factory. I must have retained more information than I thought from my father's dinner conversations because I knew a lot of historical information that I didn't even know I possessed! It was very exciting," she laughed.

Nik looked down at his hand against her softness and wasn't immune to her excitement. He swallowed hard, trying to remind himself that she was the enemy and this whole endeavor was about revenge. But her sweet innocence confused him and her excitement didn't fit the image of the calculating, two timing bitch he'd considered her after his meeting with her father.

His glance must have reminded her of what she'd done because she quickly released his hand and slid back several inches, her face looking down instead of up into his. Nik wished for that moment back but knew it was over. It was all a façade anyway, he told himself. He wasn't sure if he accepted her explanation, but he didn't care anyway. He knew she hadn't slept with either of them, Jimmy would have ensured that. As long as she didn't sleep with someone else while she was with him, that was what mattered. He would use her for his own purposes and when he grew bored, he would move on to the next woman. Her innocence or guilt was irrelevant to their relationship.

"That's great. I'm glad you were able to give them some facts and hopefully, it will steer them in your direction."

Tabitha laughed again. "I can't believe I'm just making you richer," she joked, leaning back against the leather upholstery.

Nik smiled enigmatically. "You're making yourself wealthier as well. You still own twenty-five percent of the company."

Tabitha shrugged, uncaring about her own personal wealth. It was eclipsed by his own and she'd never really cared about money anyway. She'd always known that it was the company that had held her father's primary interests. Her smile disappeared as she remembered nights lying awake, wondering what her relationship with her father would be like if the company didn't exist anymore. If she were the primary concern to him.

"What's wrong?" Nik asked softly, feeling as if the sunshine had disappeared behind a cloud now that her smile was gone. "Suddenly, you look like someone just ran over your pet cat."

Tabitha pasted a small smile on her face and looked out the window. She considered not answering him, but then turned back, looking directly into his eyes. "I was wondering what it would be like to be the world to someone," she said softly.

"What do you mean?"

Lifting one shoulder, she explained, "When I was small, my father worked about seventy hours a week. When he was home, he was usually entertaining business associates, clients or potential clients."

"And you didn't like it?"

Wistfully, she said, "I just wished that sometimes he would focus on me instead of the business."

"You don't think he was doing all of that for you? To make your future more stable?"

Tabitha laughed but there wasn't any humor in the sound. "I'm sure that's how he saw it. But the reality was, I only wanted to be with him. It was the same when you…" she stopped and looked away. "Well, suffice it to say, I thought you were different," she said and struggled to not show how hurt she'd been all those years ago at his betrayal.

"You thought I'd just be your patsy and let you run all over me?" he asked harshly.

Her eyes snapped back to his, confused and hurt by his comment. "I thought you were different. I thought you were interested in me and not in money," she said wryly. Looking pointedly at the luxurious limousine, she continued, "Boy was I off the mark on that one, eh?"

Nik didn't laugh nor did he look away from her. She was hurt but he didn't understand her anger. Hadn't she sold herself to her husband? He'd seen the reports and the stock price of her father's company had rebounded after the influx of the cash. There was no doubt about it, after her wedding, MacComber Industries had received a large, multi-million dollar boost, and the only possible source was from her husband unless Edward MacComber had started gambling, which he knew wasn't the case. How could she say she wasn't interested in money?

Since he wasn't in the mood to get into a fight, he tabled that question for later. Quickly, he considered his schedule for the next few days and made a decision he'd never have considered before. He wasn't exactly sure why he was making the decision now, especially for this woman. But he went ahead, knowing he'd regret his offer later. "If you could do anything in the world right now, what would you do?"

Tabitha laughed, startled by his question after such anger only moments before. "Sure. Just create a fantasy for the little woman, and then drag her off to another city where you spend eighteen hour days in meetings to make a few more million. Is that it?'

"No, that's not it," he countered. "What would you do?" he asked, just as the limousine pulled up outside the palazzo.

Tabitha's smile softened as she considered all of her long ago dreams. "I'd go skiing. I've never done that before but my friends all say it is wonderful," she said a moment before the door to the car was opened. She exited in front of Nik, feeling self-conscious of him behind her. But she walked tiredly toward his suite of rooms, feeling grateful for his arm around her waist, helping her walk up the steps. She felt bone tired but was afraid Nik would expect more sexual favors tonight.

She washed her face and brushed her teeth, pulling on a sexy negligee before slipping between the sheets. She heard him on his cell phone but he was talking in a foreign language so she had no idea what he was saying. She knew he was watching her as she laid down on the pillow and Tabitha desperately tried to keep her eyes open, enjoying just the sight of him with his tie off and his jacket on the chair. The first few buttons of his tuxedo shirt were undone and he looked like a male model. The man definitely knew sexy, she thought moments before her eyes closed and she fell into a deep sleep.

Chapter 7

Tabitha woke the following morning to sunshine streaming over her face and talking in the distance. It was Sunday morning, she thought to herself. They were in Florence. And Nik hadn't woken her up last night. Sitting up in bed, she looked at the pillows. There was one very close to where she was laying, indicating that he had slept next to her. And she would have sworn he pulled her into his arms at some point, feeling the strength of his arms around her and his muscular body against her back. But she was alone, except for the distant talking.

She got out of the bed reluctantly, wishing she could sleep for another twelve hours and avoid the confusion her life had become since Nik had walked back into it. But she'd never been one to avoid problems and now wasn't the time to start. Slipping her arms into the matching silk robe, she padded barefoot toward the sound of the voice she could hear.

Eventually, she found Nik sitting on the balcony of the master suite, a cup of coffee in one hand and a cell phone in the other. The newspaper was spread out over the table, parts of it on his lap and he had written several notes in the margins.

When she walked out, he looked up and winked at her, waving her into the seat across from him as he continued to talk in fluent Italian. A few moments later, he ended the call, placing the cell phone to the side while he folded the newspaper up. "How did you sleep?" he asked.

"Very well, thank you." She said stiffly and self-consciously. "And you?"

Taking a sip of coffee, he watched her over the rim. "Not so well," he replied. "I wanted to wake you up each time you moved last night, which was often."

Tabitha blushed, understanding now that he had slept with her just as she'd thought when she'd woken earlier. She'd been curled up in his arms all night and he hadn't woken her as he had the previous nights. "Why didn't you?" she asked, curious and just a little worried.

"Because you looked exhausted." He chuckled as he watched her face turn pink. "I only need about four or five hours of sleep each night. You're going to have to learn to sleep in each morning, or catch an afternoon nap in order to keep up with me," he said. "Would you like some coffee or orange juice?" he asked abruptly.

Tabitha grasped onto any change of subject. "Coffee would be wonderful," she said and leaned forward to pour it from the silver carafe on a side table. "I'll get it," she said.

"Louis will get it," he countered and a man in a white uniform appeared as if by magic and poured her coffee, putting in lots of cream and sugar, just as she liked it. How the man knew that, she had no clue, but she was grateful for the energy charged beverage.

"Would you like anything for breakfast?" he asked.

"Nothing right at the moment," she said politely, sipping her coffee. "Where are we off to today?" she asked.

"Nowhere," he said. "What about if we look around Florence? I'll take you to my favorite restaurant and just relax today."

Tabitha's eyes widened. "You do that?"

He looked at her teasing expression and almost laughed. "What do you mean?"

She smiled mischievously. "You take the day off and just relax?"

Nik's eyes sparked as he understood her teasing. Over the rim of his coffee cup, he paid her back, "Well, we can relax most of the day. But I'll definitely have you make up for your exhaustion last night," he replied and was rewarded for his efforts by seeing her cheeks instantly turn red. His soft laughter only heightened her color.

"Well, I guess that's more than I was expecting," she said, breathing slightly erratically now. The excitement was pouring through her system and she wasn't sure if it was because of the promise of sex with him, or the idea of spending an entire day with him going through the museums and highlights of Italy, just as she'd wanted to do the previous day.

To hide her excitement from him, she stood up and said, "I'll go shower then." She hurriedly walked off the balcony, taking her coffee with her.

Tabitha knew she was hiding but couldn't help it. The man completely confused her. She wanted to remind herself that he was the bad guy here but he wasn't acting like the bad guy. He was being nice and extremely considerate. Why?

She turned on the shower and slithered out of the silk negligee. The water felt wonderful and she turned her face up to the spray, then turning the jets so they were a massage and allowing the water to pound away the stress that had suddenly come into her shoulders.

Her eyes were closed and her back facing the door so she didn't hear or see Nik when he walked into the shower. Suddenly his hands were on her back, rubbing the tense muscles. When she tried to turn and face him, he kept her still. "Don't turn," he said, his voice husky.

He pulled her back against him and she could feel the evidence of his arousal against her back. Just as suddenly as the stress had come into her muscles, the stress left and a new tension entered. This one she understood and Tabitha was more than willing to follow his instructions as she allowed her hands to drift onto his thighs. Did she dare go higher? Tentatively, her fingers moved higher and since her back was to him, she dared.

Yes, she thought and let her fingers touch his erection. She wasn't confident enough to hold it but allowed her fingers to tentatively touch, to explore.

Suddenly, she was whipped around and Nik took her hand in his and wrapped her fingers around him. She stared at his face, more turned on than she could believe by the simple action. He showed her how to move, to rub her hands along the length but she wanted more. She leaned forward and tasted his chest with her tongue, sure he was going to push her away. But instead, he pulled her closer, his hand tangling in her wet hair and she felt free to taste and explore, her other hand coming up to run along his well-defined muscles as she moved down his body, exploring him.

Tabitha could barely stand but she wasn't going to let herself fall into a puddle of desire at his feet now that she had discovered that he wanted her to touch him. Both her hands were touching and her mouth tasting while his own hands covered her back, her arms, sliding along her wet-slicked body and making her writhe in need.

Suddenly, she was turned around again and before she had a chance to cry out her protest, her hands were placed on the wall of the shower and Nik's hands ran sensuously down her body, stopping at her breasts to tease the nipples, then down her waist, to her stomach and Tabitha couldn't speak much less protest. When his hands found her center, she did cry out, and yet again when she felt him press into her from behind. This was so different from before and she threw her head back, completely out of control now.

He wouldn't let her take her hands off the wall while his own came back up to her breasts as he moved inside her, then slid down to tease her again. When she climax this time, she was so out of control she was unaware of anything except finding her own fulfillment, unsure of whether Nik came or not.

When she could open her eyes again, she was being held gently in his arms, the warm water spraying down on both of their bodies as his hand rubbed her back and he kissed her gently on the lips.

"That makes up slightly for you falling asleep on me last night," he teased.

Tabitha blushed painfully and hid her face in his chest, feeling as well as hearing his rumble of laughter. "I can't believe I did that," she whispered, embarrassed now that the passion was spent.

He continued to laugh and said, "I hope you'll do that over and over again."

She peeked up at him. "Really?" she asked, worried about what he thought about her. "You didn't mind?"

In response, he took her mouth and kissed her deeply. When she was having trouble breathing again, he pulled away and shook his head. "I think I might die if you don't do that to me again," he responded.

Tabitha could see the seriousness in his eyes and was thrilled and more relieved than she could say. "Good. Because I think I feel the same way," she said finally.

True to his word, Nik took the whole day off, only answering his cell phone three or four times. He took her to all the museums and they didn't have to wait in line, apparently the Andretti machinery was well oiled and his visit organized so that he magically was given entrance through special doors and even allowed to see exhibits that weren't open to the public yet. Tabitha wondered how much one had to contribute to a museum in order to receive such special treatment, but then suspected she didn't want to know. Realization of how much Nik was really worth scared her. She didn't like knowing that he was so completely out of her league.

At dinner that night, Nik took her to a tiny restaurant that had only five tables. The food was beyond anything she'd ever had before. She had a pasta dish with a cream sauce that was filled with seafood. Dessert was the most magical white chocolate dream with fresh raspberries and a divine dark chocolate liqueur.

With each course, a different bottle of wine was served so by the end of the meal, Tabitha was feeling extremely relaxed. She suspected that Nik knew all about her mental state when he asked, "When are you going to tell me why you were still a virgin four years after your wedding night?"

Tabitha sat back in her seat, amazed that she didn't feel the rush of humiliation she usually felt when someone referred to her disastrous relationship. With a slight movement of her shoulder, she said, "Some men just aren't as impressed with my figure as you are."

Nik's expression was dubious. "I find that hard to believe," he said, knowing that she only had to walk across a room and men turned their heads to watch her.

She took another sip of wine and smiled over her glass. "Believe me," she answered firmly.

Realization came a moment later. "He was gay?" he asked.

Tabitha grimaced. "Bingo."

"Then why did you marry him?"

Waving her glass slightly in the air, she replied, "Because my father convinced me it would be in the best interests of the town and the company," she replied, her eyes looking down into her glass. "Besides, you didn't want me."

Nik's entire body tensed. "What do you mean by that statement?" he asked, his voice smooth so as not to alert her to the anger welling up inside him.

Tabitha carefully set the wine glass down on the table, not wanting him to see her fingers shake with the pain those memories created. "Let's not talk about the past. There's really no point, is there?"

Nik watched her and came to a realization that there was something missing. He just wasn't sure what that was. "I think there's every reason to discuss the past. What did your father tell you when you came home that afternoon?"

Tabitha considered her options. Looking across the table at the handsome man, she ignored the silly impulse to spill the pain out to him. But

---

she wasn't secure enough with her sexuality yet to tell him off for his awful behavior four years ago. "Let's just leave the past in the past. But there's lots to do for the future. If you're willing," she said, looking at him through her lowered lashes.

After a long moment, he allowed himself to be led down the pathway although he was determined to get to the bottom of the past at some point. A sixth sense was telling him that it was extremely important. "What do you have in mind?" he asked, smiling.

Tabitha leaned forward, unknowing that she was giving him an enticing view of her cleavage in the V neck cotton shirt. "Well, perhaps you could show me more about this sex thing that seems to be pretty nice between us."

Nik was stunned into silence for a long moment before he could speak. She wanted to have sex with him? She wasn't in this relationship simply for the company or to save her precious town? A part of him was thrilled that she was so eager for that part of their relationship. But another part of him wanted something more. That other part was ignored, not wanting to go through past foolishness again. "You'll have to explain that request in more detail," he said, wanting to make sure he wasn't reading things into her request that might not be there.

Tabitha's face fell. She had hoped that he would understand what she wanted. After this morning's activities, her discovery that there was more to sex than what she'd been experiencing the over the past seven days, and now she wanted more knowledge. Could she actually say the words? Her finger was making patterns on the red, checkered table cloth and she didn't have the courage to look at him. "I was just..." she started..." well, you know, thinking that maybe you could....teach me....." Tabitha sighed deeply, flustered and wishing she could just spill it out. She picked up her wine glass and took a long swallow of the wonderful wine, then inhaled and spilled out her request in one, fast explanation. "Like this morning, I wanted to know if you'd be willing to teach me more about sex," she whispered quickly, unable to look at him in the face so she looked off to the right, unfocused on anything except listening for his response.

Nik was quiet for a long time after that request and finally she looked up at him. He didn't look offended, or shocked or angry. In fact, he looked like a tiger who had just made a kill. The look shivered down her spine and her mouth dropped open slightly. Had she just made a very bad move, she wondered?

"Nik?" she asked, unsure of his expression.

In response, Nik stood up and took out some bills, tossing them on the table. He grabbed her hand and stood up, pulling her gently but firmly behind him as he waved to the owner on the way out of the restaurant. Of course, the limousine was waiting right outside and he pulled her into the luxurious car, right into his lap. The door closed behind them a moment before his mouth covered hers in a passionate kiss that made her ache with need.

When she was trembling in his arms, he finally lifted his head and looked down into her kiss drugged features. "Ask me that again," he said, his voice husky and his eyes on fire.

With him looking at her in that way, she had no need to fear his question. In fact, it made her bold. Reaching up, she wrapped her arms around his neck, her fingers touching the skin on his neck and his hair. "I want to know more about sex. With you," she clarified.

"Why with me?" he demanded, his hand slipping up under her shirt and touching her skin, his fingers splaying across her flat stomach making her inhale sharply.

"Because you make me feel wonderful. But you already know that."

"Any other reason?" he asked, moving his fingers along her rib cage.

Tabitha closed her eyes and licked her lips that were painfully dry. Nodding her head, she admitted, "Yes."

"What's that other reason?" he asked when she failed to continue.

"I want you," she said.

"Not good enough," he said roughly, his fingers slipping higher. "Tell me," he demanded.

Tabitha moved, wanting his fingers to touch her nipple but when she arched her back, his fingers moved out of range and she had to grit her teeth in frustration and yearning. She tried to move closer to him, to feel his chest against her aching nipples, but he held her away, knowing what she wanted and letting her feel that it was only inches away from her. When she understood that he wasn't going to give her what she wanted until she told him the truth, she gave in. "You're the only man I've ever wanted to teach me anything!" she almost yelled.

With a growl, Nik ripped her shirt, tearing off the lacy bra she had underneath and covered her nipple with his mouth. The heat seared through Tabitha and she gloried in the feelings, knowing that eventually, he would get around to putting out the flames that were already tearing at her insides.

Within minutes, they were pulling up outside the palazzo and Nik took off his jacket to drape around her shoulders, then swung out of the car before Jimmy could open the door for them. He didn't wait for her to walk, but simply lifted her into his arms and carried her up the stairs to the bedroom.

Laying her on the bed, he tossed his jacket out of the way, then stripped her skirt and underwear off. "Say it again," he demanded as he pulled the shirt off his shoulders, then tossed his pants and silk boxers out of the way. Standing there naked, looking down at her, Tabitha thrilled to the man and his features. "I want you," she said, reaching out to touch him tentatively on the chest. She sat up to get a better feel and was able to use both her hands, her fingers touching the skin, the hair and reveling in the muscles underneath. "You're so handsome," she said, her mouth reaching out and kissing him in the middle of his chest. She then nibbled and tasted, feeling everywhere and loving the fact that Nik allowed her to do this.

"I can't hold out much longer," Nik groaned and pushed her back against the bed. His fingers moved down her skin and found her core. "You're so wet for me," he said, his eyes ablaze as he entered her quickly, feverishly.

Tabitha was so turned on by feeling his body, touching and tasting that she came almost as soon as he entered her. Nik was not far behind. Afterwards, they lay together in the mussed sheets, their breathing heavy and simply held each other.

Tabitha, feeling very amorous, curled up next to him, smiling as his arm pulled her closer. "That wasn't the lesson I was going to teach you," he said, still breathing heavily.

She laughed and propped her arm up onto her hand. "What was it you wanted to show me?" she asked, her eyes laughing merrily at him, feeling very powerful that she could make this strong man want her so much.

The next several hours answered her question. Tabitha learned more that night than she ever could have imagined. Nik was the ultimate lover, relentless and controlled up to a certain point. That point was usually when she started touching him back and he lost all the control he was trying to savor as he tortured her with his lovemaking.

Chapter 8

Tabitha woke the following morning to the bright sunshine and a smile. Looking over at her bedside table, she saw the flowers instantly and her smile grew wider. It would have been nicer if Nik had stayed, but the flowers were a nice touch. Reading the note, she almost laughed out loud. "More lessons to come," was all it said.

She jumped out of bed and showered, dressing in a pair of casual slacks and white shirt. She had no idea what to do with herself, but she supposed she could do more sightseeing. She made sure her phone was in her purse and then headed out the door. With Jimmy's guidance, she strolled through museum after museum of beautiful art. Jimmy showed her galleries that were off the beaten track.

At lunch, she forced Jimmy to sit with her instead of sitting two or three tables away as he normally would do. She asked him questions about his personal life and, he was shy initially, but then started speaking about the woman he was seeing and how she was frustrated with his working hours. Tabitha asked him if he'd explained this to Nik and requested a different position, but Jimmy looked horrified at the idea. She tucked away that little piece of information for the future, not sure she could do anything to help the man. But she liked Jimmy and he deserved something more than just trailing around after her each day.

Nik called in the late afternoon and asked her if she would meet him for dinner that night. Tabitha was thrilled on two levels. First, she was excited to see Nik although still a little shy after all the things he introduced her to last night. Would he think she was wanton? The little flutters in her stomach told her she didn't really care as long as he liked her that way, which she suspected that he did.

The second side of the equation is that he was actually asking her to dinner. It wasn't a demand as it had been in the past few days. What was changing between them? She no longer felt anger toward him either. Was she willing to just ignore the past and what he did to her?

An interesting question occurred to her as she sat in the back of the car being driven home. Could there have been some confusion between what had happened all those years ago? Could her father have misunderstood the situation? She recalled the conversation she had with him, explaining that Nik had proposed to her and his intentions hadn't been the horrible things he'd said Nik had demanded. She wasn't sure how there could have been confusion, but she kept that hope alive.

Rushing into the palazzo, she hurried up the stairs and into the shower, wanting to change into something more appealing than slacks and a plain shirt. She wanted to dazzle him tonight. Considering her new wardrobe, she thought about what she could wear as she let the warm water cascade down her body.

"Oh, hello," a husky female voice said from the other side of the room. "And who the hell are you?" the strange woman demanded of Tabitha.

Tabitha, dressed only in a towel since she was still considering her options, stared at the lovely blond woman wearing a satin slip dress and almost nothing else. She was stunningly beautiful and Tabitha felt gauche and silly without makeup. Even if she'd been dressed to the nines, Tabitha could never compete with this woman's sultry beauty and style.

"I'm Tabitha. Who are you?" she asked, her hands reaching up to make sure the knot of her towel was secure. "And what are you doing in here?"

The woman smiled. "I'm Noreen. You must the upstairs maid. Be a good girl and finish getting dressed before Nik comes home. Otherwise, I'll have to tell him you've been fooling around while he's out."

Tabitha wanted to scream in anger as a flash of jealous rage sank into her bones. Nik was seeing this woman while at the same time maintaining her as a live in mistress? How dare he!

With as much dignity as she could muster, Tabitha walked calmly into the closet and pulled on some clothes. Before, she had been considering donning a cocktail dress, something flashy and interesting that she could easily take off once Nik had eaten enough food and was ready for something different to satisfy his hunger.

But knowing that another woman, someone who obviously knew the pass code to the security system installed within the palazzo, was sitting in Nik's bed waiting for him, well she just couldn't stomach that. She was livid and hurt and her chest ached where she didn't think there were muscles. Defining that she hurt around her heart would mean that she'd fallen for the man twice and that would be too much for her to endure.

No, better to get out while she still had the chance. If Nik wanted that woman, which obviously he did since he'd given her the code to come and go as she pleased, then Tabitha would not fight for a two timing, heartless bastard.

The fastest clothes were a pair of jeans and a V neck cotton shirt. She didn't even bother to brush her hair, just pulled it up into a messy pony tail before slipping a pair of tennis shoes on, not even bothering with sox since she couldn't see anymore. The tears were blurring her vision and her sniffles were making it hard for her to breathe.

"Have a wonderful night," Tabitha said, then wished she hadn't looked in the woman's direction. She was no longer dressed but was completely naked under the sheets.

"Don't worry," the woman sing-songed. "I'm planning on it."

Tabitha rushed out of the room and down the stairs. The palazzo was huge and she was almost out of breath when she ran into the foyer to grab her purse. She still had plenty of money since Nik had given her so much that first night. She was just reaching for the door when it opened on her and her worst nightmare came true. Nik was standing in the doorway, looking down on her curiously.

"Tabitha? What's wrong?" he asked, reaching for her arms when he realized that she was crying for some reason.

She shrugged out of his embrace, angrily shunning his touch. "Don't touch me!" she yelled, wiping her cheeks with her hand. "Don't ever touch me again! I might be responsible for hundreds of people's livelihoods, but there's no way I'm sharing a bed with that woman!"

"What the hell are you talking about?" Nik demanded, his hands on his hips.

"Noreen," Tabitha sneered. "She's all primed and ready for you." Tabitha hated that he was seeing her tears but couldn't stop them flowing down her cheeks. She wiped furiously at them but desperately needed a tissue for her nose. She had nothing and having him see her in such a state was humiliating.

"Who?"

"You're girlfriend, Noreen!" Tabitha yelled back, no longer able to control her temper. "How could you do that? I know that we have our differences but to throw another woman at me! That's low even for you!" Tabitha sobbed and hid her face in her hands. "And to think, I was just starting to like you!" she cried into her hands. "I hate you now!"

Turning away from him, she covered her face with her hands, her shoulders shaking with the sobs coming from her body. "I don't care! I don't care!" she sobbed to herself, indifferent at this point that the man was standing less than a foot away from her and could see and hear everything she was saying. All she wanted was to get away from him, to find some place to hide and lick her wounds, recover from this latest assault that had come out of nowhere.

Nik took her arms in his hands and turned her so she was facing him. "Tabitha, you're not making any sense. What are you telling me?"

She pulled violently out of his hands and turned her back to him. "Noreen is upstairs waiting on you."

Nik sighed heavily. "Tabitha, the only Noreen I know about is the receptionist at the Paris offices. Why would she be upstairs in our bed, naked or otherwise here in Florence?"

Tabitha closed her eyes. "I don't know and I don't care. I just want your assurance that you won't start selling off the factory parts. As far as I can tell, you reneged in the deal. I lived up to all the standards you set. And now I want out."

"Like hell!" he said and took her arm in his steel grip. "Let's just get to the bottom of this," he said, pulling her along behind him as he walked back to their bedroom. She didn't want to go, but he was too strong and pulled her all the way back up the stairs and into the bedroom they had shared for the past few days.

Opening the door, he stopped suddenly. "Noreen, I presume?" he asked, standing in the doorway.

Her smile was one of triumph and capitulation and it made Tabitha's skin crawl. "Of course! I thought I might surprise you," she said, laughing with her sexy voice.

The nerve of the woman, Tabitha thought and tried to pull away. She wanted to run and hide, furious with both herself for feeling such pain and betrayal at this turn of events that she had known from the beginning would happen. And also with Nik who didn't have the staying power to be with one woman for long and didn't have the courtesy, for the second time, to tell her to her face that he was tired of her and ready to move on to the next woman.

Nik gritted his teeth but wouldn't let go of Tabitha's arm. "And now, you can get the hell out of my bed, then hand in your badge. You no longer work for me," he said with deadly menace.

Tabitha's startled eyes snapped up to look at the woman's face. Noreen was not taking this well, Tabitha noticed. "What? But I thought…"

He glared back at Noreen's features, his face showing his anger and outrage. "You thought wrong! Good grief woman, all I did was say hello to you one time several mornings ago and you thought that was a come on? So you rushed over here to Italy and stripped for my titillation?"

The woman who had seemed so beautiful and composed several minutes ago now looked awful. The color had drained from her face, making her makeup look clownish against her white skin. She stammered and Tabitha could tell that her mind, obviously not used to being forced to think very often, was frantically trying to figure out what was happening in this scenario where she was coming out the loser. "Yes, but it was a very nice 'Good morning'. I thought we'd made a connection."

Nik was livid. "Over two words?" Nik asked, raising one eyebrow. "Get out!" he snapped.

Noreen didn't need to be told twice. Her face lost what little color had been still in her cheeks as she slipped out of bed and picked up her clothes that had been draped along the end of the bed. "You don't know what you're missing!" she said, walking out angrily, her small dress barely covering her still naked form as she held it over the front of her.

Nik walked over to the bedside table and picked up the phone. "Jimmy, there's a woman who is about to leave the house. Find out how she got up here and make sure it doesn't happen again. Also, have one of the maids get up here and change the sheets in the master bedroom. They are contaminated," he said and slammed down the receiver.

Turning to Tabitha, he crossed his arms over his chest and looked down at her. "I have literally spoken two words to the woman. Are you going to tell me that you're going to walk out on more lessons simply because the woman was stupid enough to translate a morning greeting into an invitation to my bed, but still smart enough to get through my security detail?" he demanded. "Because if you do, I'll consider that outside the bounds of sanity and I *will* sell off parts of the company," he said. He pulled her closer. "You're mine, Tabitha. And I'm not going to let that idiot woman push you out of my bed or my life."

Tabitha could see the sincerity in his eyes. She felt foolish for coming to the conclusions she had. "Well, what was I supposed to think when the woman told me to get out and then climbed into your bed? She treated me like I was one of your servants being naughty. In fact," she thought back to the horrible moments after she'd left the shower, "I think she threatened to tell you I was acting inappropriately."

Nik shook his head and held up his hand when a knock came on the doorway. "Follow me," he said, allowing the maid to come in and change the sheets. He took her hand and led her down the hallway to the office, closing the door behind him.

As soon as they were alone again, he turned her around and forced her to look up at him. "For starters, you could have trusted me," he said.

Tabitha's chin went up and she shook her head. "Trust is not part of this relationship Nik. Our past precludes that kind of feeling between the two of us. And don't even try to tell me that you trust me. Because we both know that's not true. You had basically the same reaction when you thought I was trying to pick up the two men in the piazza several days ago. You just held a trump card in the form of Jimmy who assured you that I was never out of his sight. I don't have that same assurance."

She saw his jaw tense but he shook his head. "I'm not letting you go. We'll learn to trust each other, one way or another."

"That's not fair," she yelled, taking several steps out of his reach, grateful when he allowed her some space. "You're holding all the cards here and blackmailing me."

"I never claimed to be fair. I only claimed to want you in my bed. On my terms and until I was tired of you. And I haven't reached that point yet," he said and eliminated the space he'd just allowed her as he pulled her into his arms.

She squirmed frantically but knew it was no use. He wouldn't let her go until he was ready and he had the superior strength to do what he wanted. "Let me go," she cried, turning her face away as he bent to kiss her.

"No," he said and kissed her neck instead, nibbling on the soft, sensitive flesh behind her ears.

Tabitha could have endured a forward, angry assault. What she couldn't fight against was his softness, his tender touch as he found each of her pulse points, each of the places on her body he'd discovered would drive her wild. "What was it you said a few minutes ago?" he asked her, his voice close to her ear, making her shiver with need.

"Stop, Nik," she pleaded, but there was no heat in her voice. She was still holding her purse in front of her but it was defensive now instead of angry.

His arms caressed her back, massaging the tense muscles and he pretended to think about her previous words. "I believe you said something along the lines of starting to like me," he quoted.

She shook her head frantically. "I was lying," she denied. "Remember, no trust." She gasped when his teeth nibbled her earlobe, then moved down to her collar bone, testing the area for sensitive places he had not discovered yet. "You can't believe anything I said earlier. It was all said under extreme emotion," she countered but her head fell back, giving him better access to her neck.

Nik chuckled against her flesh, the vibrations traveling along her body, sending shivers down her spine. "I'll pick and choose what I want to believe. And I think I like the fact that you're starting to like me," he said. "There's no point in denying it because I heard you say it."

"I don't! I lied earlier. As I said, it was under extreme duress. That woman caught me off guard so anything I said was completely off the record," she gasped as his hand slipped the zipper down her jeans. "Stop it, Nik," but the only heat was from wanting him and she dropped her purse as her arms wrapped around his neck. She heard the snap on her jeans and felt the fabric slide down but her arms were caught around his neck. She looked up, wondering how her arms had wrapped around him. Her mind told her to pull her arms down, to push him away. But her body didn't obey those directions. They were too absorbed in the feelings he was initiating within her.

"Stop this?" he asked, nibbling on her ear lobe as his hands pushed her jeans down her slender hips, pooling at her feet. He picked her up and carried her to the large chair situated in front of his desk. "Or stop this?" he asked, pulling her up against his erection.

Tabitha was frustrated that he was still fully clothed, even wearing his tie, while she was ready for him, needing him immediately, desperately. This was definitely a lesson that would be short and quick, she knew. She wanted him, he was going to have to lose some of the clothing. Forgetting about the events of an hour ago, she looked around at her surroundings, then realized she didn't care that they were down in his office instead of appropriately in a bedroom. She needed him now, she wanted him to validate their relationship in the most basic way possible.

"Shut up," she gritted out and pulled his tie off, then ripped his shirt, the buttons pinging against the wall somewhere. Her mouth found his chest, nibbling his skin, tasting and driving him just as wild as he was driving her. Within moments, he was out of his clothes and she was straddling him on the chair, his heat sinking into her body and his hands clutching her hips, showing her the pace that would satisfy them both.

That weekend, to Tabitha's surprise, Nik took off from work for three full days. He flew her to Switzerland and taught her to ski. They were three blissful, fun filled days with nights of passion and more laughter than she could have believed possible with a man so intimidating. His patience on the ski slopes was amazing as he endured her awkwardness with the new sport. In the evenings, he continued his lessons to the point where Tabitha felt as if she were completely under his power.

And each morning as she woke up in his arms, she stared at his handsome face, her heart melting a little more with each moment she spent in his company. She couldn't believe that he'd given her such a sweet gift. He could have just presented her with jewelry or more clothes, which is what she suspected was his usual modus operandi. But instead, he'd taken the time to be with her. To really be with her, without the constant pressures of his work interfering. It was more than anyone in her life had ever given to her and her heart twisted with both the pleasure of his gift, as well as the pain she knew would eventually come when he grew tired of her.

Chapter 9

He smelled the burning as soon as he walked into the penthouse in Paris and alarms immediately went off. Tamping down the panic, Nik searched quickly for Tabitha, eventually finding her in the kitchen, her hair tied up in a ponytail and her tongue sticking out as she concentrated on whatever was boiling over in the pot.

Nik felt a little queasy upon the realization that she was safe and sound. Leaning against the door frame, he watched her for a few moments, enjoying the view of her cute bottom in the jeans as she moved from the counter to the island, making some sort of concoction that, currently, was unidentifiable as food. "Is black smoke supposed to be coming out of the oven?" he finally asked, wondering if she was doing some sort of science experiment.

Tabitha's eager smile at his early arrival quickly disappeared when his question sunk in.

Looking over at the oven, her stomach dropped. "Oh no!" she exclaimed, dropping the wooden spoon she'd been using on the contents of the pot to rush over to the oven. Opening the door, black smoke billowed out and Tabitha had to jump back or endure affixation. "Oh Nik! What happened?" she asked, waving the pot holder to help the smoke dissipate. The smoke detectors in three areas of the kitchen started blaring and Nik couldn't help but laugh at her horrified expression.

He walked over to the stove and took the oven mitts from her, then reached into the now black pit and pulled out the pan. Looking at it curiously, he raised an eyebrow in defeat. "What was it supposed to be?" he asked.

Tabitha looked despairingly down at the charred remains of the steaks she'd tried broiling. "Well, they had been delicious looking steaks in the grocery store." Looking so forlorn he wanted to kiss her and tell her that everything would be okay, but looking at the black spots on the broiling pan, he knew there was nothing he could do to fix them to something edible. "I think the correct term now is charcoal," she moaned sadly.

Nik looked over her shoulder and grimaced. "I hate to ask, but are things supposed to be popping in the pan?"

Tabitha's mouth fell open as she turned to see what he was looking at. "Good grief!" she cried out, seeing her mashed potatoes literally popping out of the pot as if they had come alive. "How on earth could that happen?" she asked.

Nik couldn't contain his laughter as he set the broiling pan with the two black spots on it to the granite counter. "Don't ask me. I barely even knew where the kitchen was until about ten minutes ago," he stated, smothering his laughter in the face of her despondency.

He walked over to the stove and turned off the heat, then pulled the pot off the burner just to be sure it wouldn't heat anymore. Looking down into the pot, he said, "I thought mashed potatoes were supposed to be white."

Tabitha's eyes closed tightly after looking at the grayish-brown, congealed mess in the pot. "I tried baked potatoes, but that didn't work out very well either," she explained, sighing heavily. "Oh, Nik, I'm sorry. I was going to surprise you with a nice, simple meal but all I've done is make a mess of this wonderful kitchen." She sniffed, trying to keep the tears from her eyes and feeling extremely foolish.

Nik laughed and pulled her into his arms, kissing the top of her head. "I'm flattered that you would even try. How many meals have you cooked in your life?" he asked.

Tabitha sniffed. "I used to cook a lot. But after my father died, I just started heating up frozen dinners in the microwave, not bothering with much of anything. I guess I'm a little out of practice."

Nik looked at the kitchen, thinking that it looked like a hurricane had just come through. Shaking his head he asked, "Why didn't you just ask the cook to make the meal?"

Tabitha looked up at him, a blank look in her eyes before she laughed weakly. "You don't even know her name, do you?"

Nik looked down at her beautiful face and almost lost track of the conversation. "No. I don't know her name. In fact, I didn't even know the cook was a female," he said.

Tabitha shook her head at his handsome features, astonishment showing on her own face. "How can you eat someone's food and not know who prepared it?" she asked curiously.

Nik didn't give a damn about the kitchen staff. He had her in his arms and all he wanted to do was carry her off to his bedroom and make love to her. But he also liked standing here with her in his arms. And he definitely liked the fact that she had tried to cook for him. Why it was important to him, he didn't want to delve into. It just was and he was enjoying the feeling. "Perhaps because I have seven houses or apartments and I'm not very good with names."

Tabitha thought about that for a long moment then nodded her head. "Okay. I'll go along with that. To a point," she said, stepping out of his arms and taking one of the oven mitts in her hands before turning back to him, "but there's the niggling little detail that you have a photographic mind and can remember the most minute little detail. So I'm going to assume that someone else did the interviewing and hiring for your household staff and suppose that, as long as the meals are better than average, you don't interfere. Would that be an accurate statement?" she suggested, glancing at his amused face behind her as she brought the charred remains of their dinner to the sink to soak.

"That's entirely accurate," he confirmed, his eyes moving back to her bottom.

"I thought so," she sighed. "I guess you don't eat in much so it isn't really an issue."

"Good. Now explain to me why you were cooking instead of whoever it is that is supposed to cook for us?"

She smiled brightly and faced him, unknowing that there was a delightful black smudge across her cheek he didn't want to identify. "Because it is Mary's granddaughter's fifth birthday today. She was making a cake for her earlier so I sent her home to celebrate with her family."

He smiled softly down at her. "I'm guessing Mary is the cook?" he asked, not caring in the least but assuming it was important to Tabitha.

Tabitha laughed brightly. "I always knew you were very intelligent Nik," she teased.

Nik was touched by her thoughtfulness and kissed her gently. "Thank you," he said.

"You're not angry?" Tabitha asked, relieved that he didn't mind her stepping in to a situation that really didn't concern her.

"Absolutely not. If I'd known, I would have done the same."

Tabitha laughed softly. "Except for the fact that you didn't really know where the kitchen was until tonight. So how would you have known that it was a significant day in Mary's life?"

He grinned unrepentantly. "Because you just told me," he said.

"That's circular and you know it," she chuckled.

"If it gets me closer to a pizza, then I'm all over circular arguments."

Tabitha couldn't argue with him since she was hungry herself. "Good enough. I have salad!" she said excitedly.

Nik looked down at her dubiously. "Is it edible?"

Tabitha pulled out of his arms and punched him teasingly. "Only if you are nice to me," she said and moved off to the refrigerator to retrieve the bowls of salad she'd made earlier in the afternoon.

Nik smacked her on the bottom as she passed by but Tabitha only glared at him. Since he wasn't looking at the time, it was wasted effort.

Thirty minutes later, they were both sitting in the television room, their feet propped up on a giant ottoman, eating pizza and watching a movie. When the pizza was gone and only the remnants of the bottle of excellent wine left over, Tabitha curled up into Nik's arms feeling content and blissfully happy as the romantic comedy played itself out on the giant screen.

Chapter 10

Nik stared out the window to his penthouse office looking out over the city of Paris. It had been six weeks since that afternoon he'd watched Tabitha walk into the board room. Six weeks of the best sex he'd ever had in his life. And six weeks of more than just sex.

He was due to fly out tomorrow morning to Greece to be with his family. There was a wedding he had to attend and couldn't get out of it. There was one thing that was more important than anything to the Andretti clan and that was family.

The hard part was, he didn't want to leave without Tabitha. But if he brought her with him, his whole family would think there was something more to the relationship than simply a woman being his mistress. Nik had never invited any of his lovers to a family gathering, knowing what everyone would assume.

But being without Tabitha for the week was unacceptable. He thought through the planned events and considered his options. Maybe he could get through the wedding by only attending the actual ceremony. He could skip the reception…no. That would not be permitted by his mother and father, both of whom were very excited to see him. He'd been traveling for several months running the Andretti empire and he owed it to them to attend more than just the wedding ceremony. There were events starting tomorrow afternoon all the way through until the following Sunday. Six days away from Tabitha? No!

He hated feeling this trapped, wanting to break free from the hold she had over him. But each night when he came to her, no matter what city they were in, when he walked in to the house, she rushed into his arms, her smile brighter than the sunshine in his mind. He'd been leaving work early, working only twelve hours days instead of his normal eighteen to twenty, just so he could have dinner with her or wake up in her arms. He'd taken more time off in the past month than he'd taken off....well since that week he'd spent in England.

Being reminded of that debacle, Nik gritted his teeth and picked up the phone. He would attend all the events for the next six days and show both himself and Tabitha that he could live without her. He should be breaking things off with her anyway. His normal one or two month liaisons were the norm so stopping things now wouldn't be out of character.

"Yassou Mama," Nik said as soon as his mother came onto the line. "Ne, I'll be there," he promised, accepting that he would start the process of eliminating Tabitha from his life starting tonight. Well, perhaps tomorrow morning, he thought, knowing that she would be expecting him within the next twenty minutes. Realizing that he was cutting things close, he hurried through the end of the conversation with his mother, promising her that he'd be out to the villa as quickly as possible the next day.

Clicking off, he hurried out of his office, eagerly anticipating his evening with Tabitha. They weren't going out tonight as they had already done several times this week. He'd promised her this morning that they would have an evening alone with no social obligations. He liked that about her, Nik thought as he ducked his head into the limousine. Tabitha didn't demand that he take her to the latest and greatest shows or clubs, whatever hot spot was currently the place to be seen. In fact, he reflected as he looked out the window, she seemed to like staying home and just being with him during the evenings.

Walking into the penthouse tonight, Nik didn't feel the same sense of coming home, and he attributed that feeling to the fact that he wouldn't be seeing Tabitha for six whole nights. Again, he considered revising his plans and spending a few extra days here.

"Nik?" Tabitha called out. She came around the corner, a smile on her face and a pretty pink cotton dress that he'd never seen before. "Hi," she said, leaning against the wall.

"Hello yourself," he replied, walking forward so he was looking down into her eyes. "You look very pretty tonight," he said, liking the way her soft, creamy cheeks turned a delicate pink each time he complimented her. It also happened in bed, and usually after they got out of bed if he referred to anything they'd done in bed. That was another thing about her that he liked. She was completely uninhibited while making love, actually a tigress who was both demanding and amazingly giving. But out of bed, she pretended like nothing had happened. It was an interesting contrast, one he liked to point out whenever possible just to see her blush.

"Thank you," she replied, putting her arms around his neck and standing on her toes to kiss him.

"Ready for dinner?" he asked.

"Did you want to go out? I asked Mary to prepare something light, not knowing what you were in the mood for."

"You," he said without hesitation.

Tabitha smiled, but her cheeks still turned pink. "Well, you have me," she said, lowering her lashes and slipping a finger between the buttons of his shirt. "Any need for food?" she asked.

Knowing he'd be living without her for the next six days intensified the need for her now. "Not at the moment," he said, lifting her into his arms and carrying her up the stairs.

Tabitha was more than happy to go along with his plans, having spent the afternoon thinking about just this thing.

A long time later, Tabitha was laying on top if Nik, her heart beat slowly coming back to normal. Turning her face, she kissed the middle of his chest, smiling as the muscles contracted under her lips.

Flipping her over onto her back, Nik looked down into her soft, blue eyes. "I hate to tell you this, but I have to leave for a while. I have appointments that are going to take up a lot of time and I don't want to think about you alone. Why don't you head home for a few days to visit?"

Tabitha's face fell and she felt severe disappointment stab at her. She'd been with Nik for so long, she wasn't sure exactly what she would do without him. Turning her face away so he wouldn't see her reaction, she considered the possibilities. "Yes. I guess I could do that," she thought, wondering where he was going and what he would be doing. "What's going on?" she asked. She knew he was working on some difficult negotiations but she hadn't sensed that he was under a lot of stress. Just the opposite in fact. Over the past few weeks, she'd noticed him relaxing more and more, and with that change had come a very amusing and interesting companion. The man could talk about almost any subject.

"Just some things that will take up a lot of my time and I won't be able to see you. What will you do?" he asked, slipping a hand down her thigh.

Tabitha squirmed under his touch and smiled. "Maybe find another man who can satisfy me a little more thoroughly," she said and started rolling out from under him. Tabitha squealed and giggled when she found herself flat on her back once again, Nik looming over her with serious intent in his eyes.

"You think I can't satisfy you?" he growled, capturing her hands over her head and bending down to nibble on her neck.

Tabitha sighed, already ready for his next possession, her body demanding that it happen soon. "Well, I find that, with my current lover, as soon as he's satisfied me once, I want him again and again. There's just no end to the need I seem to have for him and his body."

Nik instantly released her arms and covered her mouth with his, the kiss tender but still possessive while his hands brought her body to a fever pitch all over again. In the end, he did satisfy her. And several more times that night.

Chapter 11

Tabitha rubbed her eyes, feeling exhausted after reading through so many documents. She was sitting in her father's old office at MacComber but all her thoughts were centered on Nik, wondering what he was doing, what he was thinking. Would he finish his business early? As soon as her mind traveled down that path, she stopped it, not wanting to be disappointed. It was only two days since she'd seen him and already she missed him painfully.

Sighing, she put down the latest invoice and swiveled around in the huge leather chair. Staring out the window, she thought about how things had changed over the past several weeks. Who would have thought that fateful morning that she would be sitting here contemplating her love for Nik?

Tabitha sat up straight, shivering with a sudden chill. Love? "No," she whispered. But as she thought about her relationship, she acknowledged that it was real love. And just as it had been four years ago, it was not a fleeting emotion. Four years ago, she had married a man, uncaring of her future in any way, just walking around life in a haze of pain after Nik had broken her heart. She remembered the day her father had told her she was getting married. The idea had been just as monumental as having coffee for breakfast versus tea. If she were to be married, it would have the same effect on her day if she were to go to the grocery store. Nothing had broken through her agony. Until the night of her wedding when she realized that some other man was going to touch her. Even that hadn't been as awful as realizing that he didn't want to touch her. The double rejection was beyond her ability to deal with and she'd retreated into a cocoon, forming a hard shell around herself that no one could penetrate. She wasn't even sure anyone tried.

It had been more than a year before she'd smiled. She knew that for sure because someone had commented on it. Sure, it had been a terrible year, Nik's betrayal, Jerry's rejection then his death quickly followed by her father's heart attack. Somehow, she'd survived that year but recovery had been slow in coming.

Now, knowing Nik so much more intimately, both physically and intellectually, she would have that much more to deal with once their relationship ended.

And she knew it would end. That was inevitable. Nik was not the marrying kind and she was. Nik would move on to another woman, and where would that leave Tabitha? It had taken a year to get over him the last time and she'd known him for barely a week. She'd been with Nik for almost two months, did that mean it would take her eight years to find a way out of her pain this time?

She wasn't sure of the answer, but she also knew that she wouldn't trade this time with Nik for anything in the world. Nik made her happy. They laughed and talked and made love like there was no tomorrow. He would take her slowly at times, and other times, it would be a passionate onslaught. Other times, she would seduce him, making love to him on her terms. She wasn't sure which she liked the most.

What was she going to do about the situation? Tabitha picked up a pencil and tapped the eraser against her nose, considering her options. She could break it off with him now and start the recovery process. There was always the issue of his revenge but something inside her told her that he wouldn't hold MacComber hostage anymore.

Thinking about that option, she knew it wasn't what she really wanted. And if Nik even showed up, she knew she'd fall into his arms, desperate for anything from him.

Knowing that, she understood that the only real option was to stay with him for as long as the roller coaster went on.

Her cell phone rang near her elbow and she picked it up, smiling when she read the caller's name. "Hello!" she said.

"Tabitha?" Nik's voice asked.

"Were you expecting someone else to answer?" she joked.

Nik chuckled. "Not really, but with you I'm never sure of anything," he replied.

"Well, it is me," she said cheerfully, her heart filling with excitement at the sound of his voice. "What can I do for you, sir?"

"Oh, if only you were right here to ask me that. I'd definitely show you what you could do for me."

Tabitha laughed, a warm feeling washing over her at his words. "Well, you're the one pushing yourself harder than most humans could endure."

"That brings up a very good point. What are you doing right now?" he asked.

"Reading board meeting notes," she said, wrinkling her nose although he couldn't see it. "Not very fascinating but definitely educational."

"Want to take a break?" he asked.

Only if he was going to be with her, she thought to herself. But she didn't say that, knowing that Nik would run the other way if he suspected how deeply she needed him and wanted him in her life. "What did you have in mind?" liking the way that phrase sounded just a little stand-offish.

"I can get away from this thing early tomorrow. Meet me?"

She tried to hide the excitement in her voice and said as casually as possible, "Sure. Where?"

Tabitha heard the smile in his voice as he said, "Just let Jimmy take you there. I'll see you tomorrow morning," he replied mysteriously and hung up the phone.

Tabitha laughed and folded her cell phone, wondering what she should pack. But why in the world would she worry about that? Nik's ever efficient PA had probably already phoned the maid in the London penthouse and told her what should be packed for the trip.

Sure enough, thirty minutes later, she heard the helicopter blades in the distance and looked out the window to see Nik's helicopter flying low, ready to land. A knock on the door sounded a moment later and Jimmy opened the door. "Are you ready?" he asked, his big body halfway in and halfway out, not willing to disturb her if she was still working.

She had gotten Nik to give Jimmy some help so now there were two body guards that rotated watching out for her. The other man, Diego, was just as tall and brawny as Jimmy, but not as friendly. So Tabitha liked it better when Jimmy was with her. But she also knew that Jimmy loved having the extra free time to be with his family.

Tabitha was already packing up some documents, eager to be with Nik again. "I sure am. I just got off the phone with our illustrious employer but he wouldn't tell me where we were going. Are you going to give me a hint?" she asked, excited despite herself over the mystery.

Jimmy shook his head, a slight smile on his face which was as much emotion as he would allow to come through. Apparently it was a big deal in the body guard industry to maintain a stiff face at all times. "I was told not to let you know until we were almost at our destination."

Tabitha sighed and shook her head. "Just as I thought. Loyal no matter what, eh?" she teased.

She followed Jimmy out the door and into the helicopter which took off only moments after she was seated.

By the next morning, she was standing at the door to a winter cabin, the bell hop opening the door and carrying her luggage inside. Jimmy tipped the man who disappeared quickly. Tabitha looked around, wondering how long it would be until Nik arrived. She didn't have long to wait. She had just moved up the stairs to look around when she heard the door to the cabin open and close. Running downstairs, she threw herself into Nik's arms, her mouth covering his and her legs wrapping around his waist. She didn't even blush when she felt his hands cover her bottom while he carried her back up the stairs and into the master bedroom.

The day was out of a fantasy to Tabitha. She and Nik were ravenous for each other but finally made it out to the ski slopes by the middle of the afternoon. Tabitha was only a novice skier but after the last time they'd been skiing, she was determined to do this on her own.

At her insistence, Nik took off to the black diamond runs, promising to be careful and not break his neck. Meeting him at the bottom several hours later, they ate a delicious meal at the lodge, then drank champagne in the hot tub of the cabin, savoring each other's company and talking about everything and nothing at all. Curled up in Nik's arms that night, completely satisfied in both body and mind, she smiled in the darkness, accepting that she wouldn't have traded this day for anything in the world, even knowing that Nik would eventually move on to another woman.

Back in Dorset the following day, Tabitha threw herself into socializing with her friends, walking through the factory and taking notes on things she thought might need improvements or repairs. She talked with as many people as she could, discussing ideas from all levels of MacComber industries, trying to come up with a plan to expand the company if at all possible. She wasn't sure if she would have the time to do anything about it, but the more she thought about it, the better the idea became in her mind. Why shouldn't the factory expand?

She spoke to Nik that night about the idea and they discussed it for over two hours. Nik gave her several areas to explore, already thinking along the lines she'd traveled down during the day. She was amazed all over again with his intelligence and business sense. The man was a walking textbook, she thought, curling up in bed that night with the phone tucked close just in case he called her the following morning.

Chapter 12

Nik gritted his teeth and forced another smile, enduring yet another elderly woman regaling him with her amazing daughter's wifely attributes. Nik didn't want to hear about the silly women. He wanted to escape and get out of this place and head back to Tabitha. As he accepted the bourbon the waiter had obtained for him, he smiled politely and looked around for an escape. Seeing his father, Christophe Andretti, across the room, he sent him a signal. The signal was acknowledged and accepted and Nik was relieved when a servant appeared several minutes later with a note.

Nik opened the sealed envelope and smiled, then gracefully excused himself from the irritating woman's clutches. Making his way along the pool that was decorated with floating flowers and candles, Nik smiled politely at the guests but determinedly made his way out of the patio area. Slipping down the darkened hallway, he finally found the sanctuary he had been searching for.

His father's soft laughter was welcoming. "Not a laughing matter, father," Nik said with irritation. "That was the sixth offer of marriage I have received since I arrived," he said, sighing gratefully as he sank into the leather chair in front of his father's desk.

"Well, if you would marry one of them, then it would all be over," he said, raising his glass to take a sip, watching his son over the rim of his glass. "That would be tragic though."

Nik's startled glance was caught by his father's. "Why is that?" he asked, his muscles tensing in anticipation of his sire's too knowing comment.

"Because the woman you really love would probably be devastated and you would be miserable because your wife is not your lady love."

Stunned by his father's perceptiveness, he feigned ignorance. Nik finished bringing the glass to his lips and took a long sip. "I don't know what you mean."

Christophe smiled and shook his head. "It is one thing if you are unwilling to admit your feelings to me. It would be another, far more terrible issue, if you are denying your feelings to yourself." The man took a cigar from the humidor and offered one to his son. "What is her name?" he asked curiously.

Nik shook his head at the offer of the cigar and looked down at the rich, brown liquid in the crystal glass and smiled. "Tabitha," he replied with only the slightest hesitation at revealing her name to his father. He couldn't deny his feelings any longer. If his father could see them, then it had to be bad.

Nik watched his father smile in satisfaction at the knowledge that he had been correct yet again. "And what are you going to do about this woman?"

Nik shook his head. "Nothing," he said.

Christophe's startled expression was not missed by his son. "Why not?" he demanded. "It is past the time for you to find a wife and marry her. You have obligations to your family. You have to produce and heir, Nikolai. You've known that all your life."

"Yes. And I'll find a wife. It just won't be Tabitha," he said firmly.

"But why?"

Nik wasn't sure how to explain. "Tabitha and I have a….past together."

"That's good. All couples should have a past. History is what makes us stronger, keeps us grounded."

Nik nodded his head, accepting his father's words as true but knowing that there was more to it that he wasn't willing to divulge, even to his sire. "I agree, if that past is solid and honest. That's not the case with Tabitha."

"Then why are you with her?" he demanded. "You should finish with her and find yourself a good Greek wife. Someone who will be honest and true to you. And what's more important, someone who will produce grandchildren for me to spoil."

Nik laughed, feeling a rush of love for his father who was never too old to play with children, loving all of his grandchildren and spoiling them terribly. "You already have six grandchildren. How many more do you want?"

"Many many more," he said. "I want a house full of them. And when the holidays come round, I want all of them here with me. And you are not helping me with my master plan, son."

Nik smiled despite the pain he felt at the idea of someone else producing those children with him. He desperately wanted Tabitha to be the mother of his children. But he couldn't trust her. He'd done so once. There was no trust between them. She still hadn't explained about her marriage and he wasn't willing to plan a future with someone he couldn't trust. Despite his earlier resolution not to, Nik explained what had happened four years ago, amazed that he could tell the story without the anger he usually felt. Perhaps it was because he was now in control of the situation.

At the end of the tale, Nik shrugged, explaining that she was now his mistress and a perfect one at that. "But I understand my obligations to my family. Never fear, I will work on finding someone appropriate."

His father snorted at that comment. "Forget someone appropriate. Find it in your heart to forgive this woman. It sounds like you need to have a long conversation with her and find out what happened."

Nik heard the door close behind him and groaned inwardly. "I agree, my love," his mother, Stasi Andretti said. His beautiful mother walked around the chair and leaned against her husband's chair, one arm draping along his shoulder as she took the cigar and put it out in the ash tray, quietly ignoring her husband's glare. "I remember you four years ago. You lost track of reality, son. You were out of your mind with grief for whatever had happened. You love this woman although I'm not sure you're willing to admit that. And even if you are willing to acknowledge it, you don't understand the depths of those feelings for her."

Nik swirled the liquid in his glass, struggling to remain calm. He didn't like what she was saying. "You're wrong mother," he said sadly. "It won't work. There's too much distrust."

Her mother made an inelegant sound, similar to her husband's of moments before. "You're just making excuses because you are scared. Scared of what this woman makes you feel." She smiled confidently. "But I know you. You are proud, but you aren't stupid," she said, her shoulders going back imperceptivity as she said, "You won't let someone that makes you feel this way escape. It is just a matter of time before you come to your senses."

Nik smiled ruefully, knowing that he wasn't going to make the same mistake twice. "I am honored that you have such faith in me, mama," he said, rising to his feet. "But I think we have a house full of guests and we should probably be more sociable."

"Pah!" her mother said, waving her hand at the idea dismissively. "You're going to be stubborn for a while. I understand. But I stand by my statement. I did not raise a stupid son. You'll find your way. I have faith in you," she said and walked out of the office, reaching up and kissing Nik on the way.

Christophe followed his wife but paused beside Nik. He stared at the door to his office before turning back to Nik. He slapped his son on the shoulders, both men about the same height and breadth. "You're going to have to give up the fight now, my son. You're mother knows about this woman although she didn't hear her name. It is only a matter of time," he said, leading the way ahead and back to the party.

Nik followed his father out but was surprised to note that he wasn't as irritated about the topic of marriage as he normally would be. Nik smiled at the idea. He definitely wouldn't marry Tabitha. No way would he marry someone he didn't trust and who didn't trust him. That was just a recipe for disaster. But at least he wasn't horrified at the idea of marriage now. That was definitely progress. Although he wouldn't tell his mother about his lack of annoyance. He'd never hear the end of the topic.

Saturday night, Nik watched as the bride and groom left the reception, both deliriously happy. Nik was glad for his cousin, but his thoughts were centered on the woman he'd been without for the past three days. He had agreed to stay in the villa with his parents until tomorrow afternoon, but he considered that he'd proven what he'd set out to prove. He had stayed away from her for long enough. Granted, he hadn't been able to do it for the full six days. Having found that he was not needed for any social obligations one of those days, he'd chosen to spend it with Tabitha. The interlude had made the rest of the parties and wedding festivities more bearable.

But as he watched the limousine carry the newlyweds off, his hand was already reaching into his pocket, preparing to order the plane fueled for takeoff tonight. There was no need to stay for the rest of the party tonight, and he could make his excuses to his parents, aunt and uncle about missing the brunch and picnic tomorrow.

He lifted the cell phone to his ear and looked across the party. His eyes were caught by his mother and father, both of whom had a glass of champagne in one hand, holding each other's hand with the other. His mother raised her champagne glass in a toast to him, her knowing eyes telling him that she understood his urgency and condoned it. Not that he would have done anything differently, he thought as he ordered the plane to be prepared to leave immediately. But it was a relief he wouldn't have to cross the throng of guests to tell them his plans.

Two hours later, Nik was on the plane bound for London and Tabitha. Closing his eyes, he tried to sleep, but his body was too primed to hold her in his arms. Once he'd touched down in the capital city, his helicopter sped his journey from the airport to the penthouse and Nik actually sighed in relief as he undressed at the end of his bed, a look of satisfaction on his face as he watched Tabitha sleep peacefully. He wasn't even surprised to see that she was wearing one of his shirts, was sleeping on his side of the bed and was hugging his pillow against her body.

Taking off his clothes, he slid between the sheets, turning her around so she was holding him instead of the pillow. Not until he had her comfortably settled against him, did he close his eyes and fall asleep.

Chapter 13

Tabitha sighed happily as she pulled the pillow on the comfortable sofa in Nik's office more securely under her back, glancing across the room at Nik as he worked at his desk, a furrow of concentration creasing his brow. She was slowly working her way through her personal bills, checking the details and making sure all of the items listed were actually purchased. There weren't many thankfully. Nik had assigned a PA to take care of most of her accounts. There were some though that she refused to allow him to pay for. They were the taxes on the house her father had left to her, the electricity bill, which was kept on only to maintain the plumbing and a few other strays that seemed to pop up. She paid for those out of the money she earned being a member of the board, which wasn't much, but allowed her a small sense of security and independence.

The letter caught her by surprise. "What?" she cried in outrage.

"What's wrong?" Nik asked, immediately looking up from the documents he'd been reading.

Tabitha barely looked up from the letter, shaking her head. "I can't believe that awful man!" she exclaimed.

Nik's expression became concerned. He didn't like her talking about another man, much less getting a letter from him. "Tabitha, what's going on?" he asked again. It was about nine thirty at night a few days after he'd come back from Greece. He was working on a contract, editing some changes he wanted while Tabitha worked on her personal finances next to him, going through correspondence his PA had been gathering for her while she traveled with him.

Her pained expression looked at him over the paper and his heart clenched. He didn't like her expression one bit. He held out his hand and she handed him the letter, her fingers shaking and her eyes tearing up before she looked away.

Nik watched her stand up once he had the letter, but she didn't go far. She crossed her arms over her chest and stood with her back to him. Looking down, he quickly skimmed the letter, trying to determine what had upset her so deeply.

"I don't understand, Tabitha. This is about your late husband? Apparently, someone else is claiming rights to his property."

Tabitha turned back to him, wiping her wet cheeks with the back of her hand as she nodded in confirmation. "You got it," she laughed but it was more of a sob than filled with humor.

Nik glanced down again, re-reading the three, short paragraphs. "This makes no sense. This person is claiming a closer relationship? But this is...." Nik looked up as understanding dawned. "A man," he finally finished. Nik shook his head. "You mentioned that he was gay. Somehow, it just didn't sink in until this moment. I'm sorry," he said, his eyes showing his sincerity.

Tabitha nodded, fighting back the tears and the old feelings of inadequacy. "He can have everything. I've never sold anything of Jerry's. I don't want anything to do with him," she said and shivered.

Nik stood up and came around his desk, taking her into his arms. He held her close, feeling her trembling. "What happened?" he asked, tensing as he prepared for her to tell him it was none of his business again. Or worse, lie to him.

Instead, she buried her face in his chest and wrapped her arms around his waist, squeezing tightly. "He was gay," she whispered. "He wanted nothing to do with me."

She'd already admitted that much to him several weeks ago. But he needed more information to make that all fit into the puzzle. "Why would you marry a homosexual?" he asked gently.

Tabitha laughed again. "At the time, I didn't care about anything."

His hands hesitated only a fraction of a second before continuing. "You didn't care that you were marrying a man who preferred men?"

She sniffed and pulled away slightly so she could wipe a tear from her cheek. "I guess you could say that but it was more. I didn't care about breathing. I didn't care about life. My father told me I was going to be married in a few days. I vaguely remember the ceremony, but I think my memories are more from the pictures I looked at two years later than from anything I actually saw or experienced that day."

"Why is that?" he asked, running his fingers through her hair soothingly.

Her hands balled into fists, clenching at his shirt. "Does it matter?" she asked, her sobs turning into genuine tears.

Nik picked her up in his arms and carried her over to a sofa. "Yes," he said. "I think it matters a great deal."

Tabitha wouldn't look at him as she said, "You didn't want me. Then Jerry didn't want me, but I didn't care about that until I slept on the floor of the bathroom on our wedding night. It was too much for me to deal with. So I just shut down. Well, actually, I'd shut down after you left me. But that's neither here nor there," she sobbed, the cries wracking her body as she spilled out all of the pain of that awful year.

"And the money? Was it worth it for the money?" he asked, not judging her anymore. He didn't understand, but deep down, he knew there was more to this situation than he'd discovered so far.

"I never saw any of the money and didn't know about it until after the wedding when I tried to get out of that horrible relationship. I'd spent a miserable two weeks in a hotel room while Jerry and his lover traipsed about the island together. When we got back, I told him that I was going to get an annulment but he threatened to demand the money back if I didn't remain with him, being his dutiful little wife and being the hostess at all his social occasions." Tabitha explained, sniffing and wiping her cheeks again. She stood up and started pacing back and forth as her mind played through the memories of that terrible period in her life.

"The money your husband put toward your father's company after the wedding," he clarified.

Tabitha nodded her head. "I hated my father after that. I know I shouldn't have. I should have gone to him and asked him to explain but I couldn't believe he would do something so horrible to me. It was a sale and he'd done something I couldn't forgive him for."

Nik didn't say anything, just waited, knowing that Tabitha was going through something he couldn't understand. He stood there, wanting to support her by just being near her, offering her his strength.

Tabitha wrapped her arms around her waist, her mind drifting back to the past. The way Jerry had treated her, like some sort of servant that owed him a service, which is exactly what had happened. She'd been sold by her father and there was no way around that fact. "My father sold me," she whispered, shivering at the memory. "The company had been in trouble. I'd known that. My father had mentioned several lost deals and was angry for the longest time. Then all of a sudden, he wasn't angry anymore. The next thing I knew, you had left and I was being fitted for a wedding dress." Covering her face with her hands, she shook her head. "Oh! How could he?"

Nik stood up and took her in his arms again, relieved when she didn't pull away. "I don't know," he said honestly. Nik couldn't understand how a man could sell his daughter in that way. He supposed that Jerry, being a businessman, didn't want others within the business community to know he was gay. But that was no excuse for Edward to have sold his daughter. He believed Tabitha's anguish was real, could feel her trembling and wanted to absorb her pain into his body, to ease the feeling of betrayal he suspected she was feeling.

"I'm sorry," he said, holding her close and rubbing her back, soothing her in the only way he knew to ease the pain.

After a long time, Tabitha sniffed and pulled away slightly but stayed within the circle of his arms, needing his warmth and strength. "I guess that explains a lot," she said. "Including the reason for my father's heart attack. There had been no indications of a health problem before my wedding. Or at least, none that he let on about. But he declined rapidly after the wedding. At the time, I was too absorbed in my own problems to think about his. And after Jerry died, I was too glad to be free of the man to even think about someone else's worries. But now, looking back, I can see how my father declined severely, quickly, after the wedding."

"What do you think caused it?" he asked, already knowing the answer but wanting her to come to the same conclusion on her own. He was still holding her in his arms, her soft scent wafting to his nose and her hair tickling his chin. He liked all of it. He liked the way she felt and the way she smelled, the way she held him. There wasn't much about the woman he didn't like, he realized. Picking her up, he carried her back to the sofa, tucking her head against his shoulder as the trembling slowly subsided.

"I think it was because he regretted what he'd done," she said softly. She wanted to hear that Nik regretted his part as well, but there was only silence. She sighed gently, knowing that she'd have to take things one step at a time. Closing her eyes, she tried to concentrate on the thoughts drifting through her mind, the past, the present, her father's motivations. But in the end, all she could do was slowly fall asleep as the emotional upheaval took its toll on her.

Nik knew the exact moment she fell asleep. He could feel her steady breathing against his chest and simply stayed just where he was, enjoying her body resting against his. It was almost midnight when he lifted her into his arms and carried her to the bed. He slowly undressed her, leaving only her tee shirt and underwear on. Undressing himself, he pulled her against his body, unwilling to leave her alone for the night. But he only held her, thinking through all the things that were said during the night.

Chapter 14

Tabitha was shampooing her hair when she heard the phone ring. She hurried to rinse her hair, but knew she'd never make it to the phone in time. Assuming the caller would simply leave a message, she finished her shower and then pulled a towel around her. Padding barefoot out of the bathroom to the closet, she considered her schedule for the day. She was planning on going shopping today. Nik had mentioned several events on his calendar, including a few charity balls. She didn't have anything appropriate for something that glamorous and had mentioned that to Nik. He laughed and told her to just pick out something from one of the magazines that she liked. He'd have the designer deliver it within a few days.

Tabitha shook her head and pulled out a simple pair of slacks and an easy white shirt. She would be in and out of boutiques all day so she might as well wear something that was easy to get into and out of.

Tabitha was almost finished brushing her hair when she heard the front door open and close. Since no one came into the penthouse without security calling them up for permission, Tabitha assumed it was Nik.

"Nik?" she called, carrying her brush out of the bedroom, smiling eagerly to see him, if a little shy after the emotions and revelations of the previous night.

Tabitha stopped short when she saw the beautiful older woman standing in the middle of the living room, placing her purse on the coffee table. Her hair was black and pulled back into an elegant chignon and she was wearing a very smart Chanel suit with matching shoes. The woman smiled when she saw Tabitha.

"Good morning," the woman said. "You must be Tabitha."

"I am," Tabitha replied, holding the brush in front of her as if it were some kind of weapon. "Forgive me for being rude, but who are you?" she asked.

The woman laughed softly and moved around the sofa so she could shake Tabitha's hand. "Forgive me for my rudeness," she was saying. "I'm Stashi Andretti. I'm Nikolai's mother."

"Oh, goodness!" Tabitha exclaimed, taking the older woman's hand nervously. "I'm sorry if I came across as crass. I have just had some odd experiences lately," she said, finishing lamely since she realized that telling Nik's mother that strange woman tended to show up naked in Nik's bed wouldn't make a very good impression.

"Nonsense," the woman said, waving her hand dismissively. "I took you by surprise. But I can say that I'm very glad to meet you," she said. She walked back over to the coffee table and picked up a stack of magazines. "Jimmy mentioned that Nik wanted you to have these. I have no idea why," she said, carrying the stack of about ten magazines to Tabitha.

She couldn't help it, Tabitha had to laugh at Nik's thoughtfulness. "Oh, well, thank you," she said, taking the heavy stack.

"What's that about?" Stashi asked.

"Nik mentioned that I would need some dresses for a gala in a few days. He said I should just look up something I liked and have the designer send it off to me."

Stashi shook her head. "Nik knows better than that. Come my dear. Let's go shopping and I'll show you how it is done," she said and walked over to pick up her purse again. "I have a feeling you and I have a lot to talk about," she smiled.

Tabitha was wary of conversing with Nik's mother. "Are you sure Nik wouldn't mind?"

Stashi gave her a secretive smile. "Nik knows nothing about my visit yet so what harm can there be?"

Tabitha couldn't come up with a way to politely get out of the shopping excursion so she excused herself to go put on some shoes.

Twenty minutes later, Tabitha was surrounded by a bevy of sales ladies who were jumping at Stashi's commands. There were hats, gloves, shoes, dresses, slacks, shirts, evening gowns, ball gowns and clothes she had no idea why she would wear them. But Stashi explained that all were absolutely necessary.

"But I only needed some gowns for a few charity events," Tabitha countered when Stashi ordered ten evening gowns, all in different colors and styles.

"Nonsense. You only need a few for the next few weeks. But Nik has other obligations and you'll need to be prepared for any eventuality."

Tabitha knew that it was time to be honest with Nik's mother. "I don't think you understand about my relationship with your son," Tabitha began slowly, cautiously.

Stashi's face broke out into a mischievous smile. "Oh, I think I understand completely."

Tabitha couldn't stop the woman and just allowed herself to be dragged from one store to another, knowing she could return many of the items after she left again.

By noon, Stashi declared a halt. "Lunch," she said and asked Jimmy to take them to the nearest restaurant.

During lunch, Stashi quizzed Tabitha about her past, her previous marriage, her schooling, where she grew up and her thoughts on marriage and children. Tabitha thought the last part was out of the realm of possibility, but she answered them honestly. By the end of the meal, Tabitha was much more comfortable with the woman and laughed easily as she heard stories of Nik's childhood with his sisters.

After the meal, Stashi said she had to fly back to Greece. She left Tabitha with a gentle hug and a huge grin, inviting her to stay with them soon.

Tabitha shook her head as Jimmy closed the limousine door behind her. "How about a stop at Nik's office?" she suggested. Jimmy immediately picked up the phone and organized the visit. The car pulled up outside the massive steel and glass building five minutes later. Tabitha was escorted up to the executive floor where she was greeted by a very efficient looking woman in her mid-fifties.

"I'm Eleanor," the woman introduced herself, extending her hand to Tabitha. "I am Mr. Andretti's personal assistant," she said. "Unfortunately, Mr. Andretti is in a meeting for a few more minutes. Would you like to wait for him? Or if it is urgent, I can pull him out."

"No!" Tabitha said quickly. "This isn't urgent. And if Nik is booked for the rest of the day, I can come back."

Eleanor smiled professionally and shook her head. "No. He doesn't have any meetings for several hours. You can wait in his office," she suggested.

"No, that's okay. I'll wait out here," she said, taking a seat on the sofa and pulling up the latest magazine on the coffee table. She was flipping through the pages when she suddenly stopped. There, staring right back at her with a handsome smile that made her stomach flip flop, was Nik. His arm was around another woman and Tabitha frowned, trying to suppress the stab of jealousy that formed in her stomach with the picture. It had to be several months old, she told herself and glanced at the cover. Tabitha's mind froze when she saw the date that revealed the magazine had just come out. Flipping back to the picture, she read the caption. Gasping, Tabitha realized that the picture was taken two weeks ago! That was the time when Nik was away, the only six days they'd spent apart in two months! Apparently, he wasn't at some awful business negotiation as she'd assumed. Nik was back home in Greece, attending a wedding of his cousin at his family's private villa. The woman on his arm looked sweet and adoring as she smiled up at Nik.

"Tabitha?" Nik's deep voice said from the hallway. "I heard you were here. Why didn't someone pull me out of my meeting?" he said, and walked over to her. "What's the surprise about?" he asked.

Tabitha fought the tears as she held out the magazine. "Today's been filled with all sorts of surprises."

"What's that supposed to mean?" he asked and took the magazine she was holding out to him. "Is there something you'd like me to read?" he asked, flipping through the pages. "Did you find a dress you liked?"

Tabitha crossed her arms over her stomach, trying to ease the heartache. But could anything help? It was four years ago, all over again. "Why are you doing this to me again?" she whispered.

Nik's eyes slashed to her face, then back down to the magazine. It took him a moment but he finally understood after reading the caption under the picture. "I think we need to have this conversation in my office," he said and reached out to take her arm.

"Don't touch me," she said harshly, pulling out of his reach. "I'm leaving."

"No, you're not," he ground out. He took her arm and pulled her into the office behind him, closing the door and leaning against it. "Now explain to me what you think this picture means," he demanded.

"Those days we were apart," she started off, "you were with another woman, weren't you?"

"No! I was at a family wedding. This picture was taken while I was getting a drink from a waiter. The woman is my family's next door neighbor. My parents might have wanted the two of us to get together but they know that's not going to happen."

Her face drained of color. "Well, that's an interesting story. I guess I'm not good enough to bring home to your parents. So in effect, you were out dining and dancing with women your parents find suitable to marry but I'm left off to the side," she said angrily. She closed her mouth for a long moment, then her eyes widened and she gasped in horror. "I'm your mistress, aren't I?" she asked.

Nik started to say something but she interrupted him. "Oh goodness! I'm the other woman. The female in the picture, she's not the one I should be jealous of, because I'm only the mistress, the one who amuses you. I have no right to be jealous, do I?"

Nik tossed the magazine onto the table, uncaring if it landed on the glass or fell to the floor. "First of all, you have to have feelings for me in order to be jealous. Are you saying there are feelings on your side?"

"Of course there are!"

"What do you feel for me Tabitha? And no more lies. I want it all on the table this time."

Tabitha stabbed him in the chest angrily as she enunciated each word with furious clarity. "First of all, I've never lied to you. Secondly, I don't sleep with people I'm not in love with."

There was a long silence as Tabitha realized what she'd just said. Her worried eyes looked up to his and she cringed at the triumph she read there.

"You love me?" he asked, wanting her to say it again.

Tabitha shrugged and turned away. "Right now, I hate you."

Nik was smiling as he turned her back to face him. "But at other times? You love me?"

She pulled away. "I don't know why I do this to myself," she said softly and Nik could hear the fear in her voice but didn't understand it. "I fell in love with you four years ago but my father told me that all you wanted from me was money. This time, you were out for revenge and it still happened." Taking a deep breath, she shook her head, "I guess I never fell out of love with you. I think I've spent the last four years waiting for you to come back and explain why you said those awful things to my father." She turned around and looked at him. "Why did you?" she asked.

Nik shook his head and put a hand on each of her arms. He wanted to pull her into his arms but knew she'd reject that kind of intimacy at this point. "I'm not sure what your father said, but perhaps you could tell me and we could get it all out into the open."

Taking a deep, shuddering breath, she closed her eyes and thought back to that horrible afternoon she'd come back from Lucy's house.

When he saw how much effort it was taking for her to discuss the past, Nik placed a finger over her lips to silence her. "Since this seems so hard for you, and you've already revealed a great deal both last night and a moment ago, perhaps I should go first." At her relieved expression, he continued, "He asked me how much money it would take to get rid of me. He also mentioned that you were already engaged and that you liked to lure men into proposing as a sign of the strength and power you had over them. You would then reject them and move on to the next man."

Tabitha's heart hurt at her father's betrayal. "That's not true," she whispered. "I've never had an offer of marriage except from you."

"And your ex-husband," he reminded her.

She shook her head emphatically. "No, he never proposed to me. It was all a business arrangement between the two of them. My father came into my room one afternoon and told me it was all arranged. I was just told when to be dressed and…"

"And you were so hurt that you went along with it?"

"Yes," she said sadly. "I didn't care about anything since you'd left me. My father told me that you had demanded money and when he wouldn't give it to you…" she stopped, unable to finish.

"That's not true either," he said softly. "I hate to belittle what memories you have left of your father, but he offered me the money to get out of your life. He said not to be greedy because there wasn't much."

Tabitha closed her eyes, trying to squeeze the pain out. "That sounds like something he would say. The man reduced everything down to a business deal and money. Human emotions were a weakness to him."

"I'm sorry I didn't trust you back then," he said softly, kissing her gently on her head.

"We'd only known each other for a week. We didn't know each other long enough to trust."

Nik shook his head. "No, I was just afraid of looking foolish. I'd never been in love before so I didn't know how to handle the emotion."

"Who was the woman after me?" Tabitha asked, not really wanting to know the answer but needing to get all the cards on the table, so to speak. She wanted no more secrets between them.

"What woman?"

Tabitha took a breath and leaned her forehead against his chest. "I called and called, probably two or three times a day for a week after you left but you never answered your cell phone. Until one day when a woman answered it. There was music and people laughing in the background."

Nik thought back to that period and considered all that had happened. "It might have been a celebration, but I wasn't really there. I was almost constantly on my cell phone so your messages probably went into voice mail. My PA checks them and prioritizes who I should call back. She was probably the person who answered the phone that day as well. There was a big celebration over an acquisition around that time. It was pretty vicious."

"So there wasn't a woman after me?"

"There were. Several, in fact," he said regretfully. "I didn't live like a monk. But I could never find someone who could even come close to replacing you. And when one woman didn't blank out your memory, I looked for another and another and tried over and over to dim your memory. But nothing worked."

Tabitha didn't understand what he was saying. "What are you trying to tell me?" she asked, wiping her tears with a tissue. Her heart was telling her that he was in love with her, but her mind, so recently hurt, was afraid to grasp at the straw.

"I'm saying that I couldn't live without you. No matter how much I tried, you were always there, never releasing me from the time four years ago when I fell head over heels for you."

"You loved me back then?" she asked.

"I loved you then and love you now."

"Then why...." She stopped, afraid to bring up the past.

"Please," he started out, his finger gently wiping away a tear that slipped past her lashes. "Don't hide from me anymore. Ask anything you'd like. I think we should have done this four years ago. We wouldn't have gone through all this hell otherwise."

Taking a deep breath, she looked up into his eyes, hope shining through. "Are you saying my father lied about you all those years ago? That you really did want to marry me? And he made up the story about the money?"

"Yes. Just as he forced you into a marriage you didn't want. He pushed me out of a marriage I did want. I wanted you very much all that time ago. Will you start again with me now? Will you marry me, Tabitha?"

Tabitha couldn't wait any longer. She threw her arms around his neck and held on with her life. "Yes! Oh, please, let's marry soon just so we don't have to worry about something happening again. I don't think I can go through that kind of hell again."

"Deal," he laughed, holding her close to him, his face buried in her hair as he breathed in her clean, fresh scent.

One month later, Tabitha took the hand of the man she'd fallen in love with more than four years ago, her love for Nik shining through in her eyes and receiving the same message in return. She couldn't take her eyes away from him, amazed at how handsome he was in his morning grey suit and tails. She always thought this would be a scary moment in her life, but when the minister cleared his throat to begin the ceremony, she was more thrilled than nervous.

"I love you," she whispered as the priest droned on about marriage and duty. The smile that formed on Nik's face when she said those words was worth more than all the money in the world.

"I love you too," he said and bent to gently kiss her lips.

The crowd laughed and cheered when the minister looked upset by their kiss, seeing as how it was out of order. He'd barely begun. Not in all his years had he seen someone kiss the bride before he'd even gotten to the vows. But then, he'd never met two people more in love, he reminded himself. Then smiled benignly at the bride and groom as the rest of the congregation settled down. He'd get them married soon enough, he thought to himself.

Excerpt from "The Billionaire's Runaway Bride"

Each day was getting easier, Sophie Randal thought to herself. This living thing was becoming less agonizing. A few months ago, taking a breath had been difficult. Blinking had hurt because her eyes were too swollen from crying and her heart ached beyond what she'd thought a heart's capacity for pain could endure.

Sophie wiped the sweat absently from her brow before pulling the hydrangea bush more to the left, centered the leaves so they were rounded in the front and then filled in the hole with soil and mulch. "There, that should leave you happy over the winter," she said to the plant, patting the mulch and gently touching the leaves. She sighed contentedly, knowing she had accomplished something today.

She was productive now, not just someone's burden. Looking at the plant, she tucked a stray lock of curly red hair behind her ear absently and, with dark blue eyes that finally sparkled with life again after months of appearing blank, looked around with satisfaction at the newly created landscape she'd been working on all day.

"This is good," she said out loud. "You're all going to be happy and healthy, aren't you?" she said, talking to herself as much as to the plants.

Unfortunately, that feeling of peace and satisfaction was to disappear with the next sound, making her heart freeze in her chest. She felt the shadow only moments before he spoke, sending a shiver down her spine in both fear and anticipation.

"Talking to plants again, Sophie?" a deep voice behind her asked.

Sophie froze as fear and incredulity intruded. It couldn't be! There was no way Jason Randal could have found her. She was even at a client's site instead of her tiny little cottage or the landscaping company's headquarters! How on earth could he have tracked her down to this upper class house in the middle of nowhere?

But then Jason had more resources than any one person had the right to have. He was wealthier than anyone else she knew with an obscene amount of money at his disposal, all personally made. He wasn't the kind of man who had inherited anything. Jason Randal had built up his massive empire by intelligence, amazing determination and, if the news reports were true, merciless strategizing.

So why wouldn't he now use those resources to find her? Unfortunately, Sophie had assumed that he wouldn't. She had, in fact, prayed that he wouldn't. Over the past few months, she had convinced herself that she was too trivial for him to waste the effort and expense. She had been hoping that Jason Randal would just forget that she even existed.

But as she considered that fantasy, she realized that she had obviously been wrong. Incredibly wrong. She'd forgotten one important detail about Jason's personality. Jason Randal didn't like sharing. And as his wife, he would want to make sure she was under his wing and acting appropriately.

Sophie stood up and turned around slowly, hoping and praying that she was wrong and that Jason Randal was not standing two feet behind her. Please let it be some other man who had the same kind of deep, velvet voice that made her insides quiver and her heart speed up with anticipation.

As she turned around, her fears were confirmed. The tall, muscular man that had invaded her dreams every night for the past six months, leaving her breathless and wanting each morning upon waking, was behind her, casually leaning against a wooden fence that was bordered by the pretty purple and yellow pansies she'd planted just an hour ago and looking more handsome than anyone should.

Her throat clenched and her eyes surveyed his broad shoulders, flat stomach and long, muscular legs all encased in a masterfully tailored suit. She knew the suit didn't have any padding in the shoulders. She knew every inch of the man's body intimately. Unfortunately, her traitorous body was reacting to merely the sight of him.

Jason's eyebrow went up, just as she'd remembered him doing whenever she'd amused him in some way. "No words, Sophie? Not even a greeting? How ungracious of you," he said and pushed off the fence to walk towards her. "What are we going to do about your manners?" he considered, taking a stray lock of her fiery red hair and wrapping it around his finger. "Ready to go home, Sophie?"

The last words broke her out of her trance and she reared back, only to be stopped painfully as the hair that was still tangled in his large hand, yanked against her scalp. "What are you doing here, Jason?" she demanded again, unwrapping her hair from his fingers, careful not to touch him in any way. From past experience, she knew that would lead to her wanting him. Humiliatingly, since he could have just about any woman he wanted with a crook of his sexy finger whereas she was a nobody, someone he'd married out of pity.

She raised her face up, determined to not cower around him anymore. She was a new person and she was finished with cowering. She'd done it for twenty-five years but when she'd walked out on her marriage, she decided it was time to stop.

"I am home," she asserted and turned away, determined to walk back to her truck and drive away.

Her retreat was stopped by a steel band that wrapped around her arm, pulling the rest of her body up against his hard frame and Sophie couldn't help but cringe. Seeing the anger in his eyes, the clenched jaw and the nerve that was ticking in his cheek, all her old fears came back to her. "You are my *wife*!" Jason said. "No wife of mine will be digging around in the dirt."

The spicy scent of his aftershave reached her and she fought hard against her longing for his incredible masculinity. She hated the insecurity that crept into her voice, but she couldn't help it. "I sent the divorce papers already. You should have received them by now," she choked out, wishing she could put just a small amount of space between her body and this angry man holding her. Jason never showed emotion! They had been married for only a short time and never during that entire time had he ever shown her any emotion other than mild amusement. But he was definitely angry now.

Her words only seemed to infuriate him more but he fought for control and won. "Ah, yes. I received them. 'Irreconcilable Differences'," he quoted, referencing the reason she'd stated for the divorce. "But I disagree my love," he replied, one finger sliding sensuously across her cheek to brush against her extremely sensitive earlobe before dropping to her waist again. "I think we can work through whatever differences you perceive as irreconcilable."

"No!" she cried, trying yet again to pull away from him. "Why? Why in the world would you want to stay married to me?" Sophie had heard too many times from her father that her hair was too wild for any respectable man to pay attention to her. The titian curls swirled around her shoulders no matter how hard she tried to subdue them with pins.

Her eyes were pretty, she knew but her skin was too white and her lips too full to be classically pretty, which were the kinds of women Jason used to date before he'd married her. She knew because she'd seen the pictures of those women, smiling in the newspapers as they walked on his arm - elegant, classically beautiful women who were confident and daring, everything she was not.

She was too thin. The only part of her anatomy that showed any sign of femininity was her large bosom which she'd learned over the years to conceal out of shame, a shame that her father had impressed upon her at the first sign of their impending bloom.

"Why wouldn't I?" he said, loosening his hold but not letting her go. "You're my wife."

Sophie's chin went up a notch as she desperately searched for the small bit of confidence she'd gained in the past few months. "You've said that but I won't do it anymore. You married me out of pity and I won't be pitied by anyone!"

Jason's hands dropped down to his sides and his hard, dark eyes looked down at her in surprise. "Pity? Why in the world do you think I married you out of pity?"

Sophie put several feet between them, rubbing her arms together although the early spring afternoon was unusually warm. Nor was it because he'd hurt her arms. Jason would never hurt her. It was more that any touch from Jason burned her skin, melting her insides and making her mind turn from whatever it had been thinking and focus only on him and the heat of his hands or body. It was a dangerous road and one she was determined not to go down. She had pride now. She wasn't going to lose it simply because her traitorous body wanted to melt into his.

"Don't worry about how I know. I just do. You don't have to hide it anymore, Jason. It was very noble of you to marry me after my father's death and show me kindness but I'm okay now. I can survive on my own."

Jason looked around her, down at the ground where the rusty tools were laying and her filthy work gloves were tossed. "Is this what you call surviving?" he demanded. "You gave up on our marriage and the position as my wife in order to live here, in this tiny village and drive that?" He waved to the ancient truck with the other gardening tools in the back.

"Yes!" Sophie claimed, not ashamed of her job or what she chose to drive. She didn't expect him to understand. Jason lived in an enormous mansion with rooms decorated by the best designers, his personal chef cooked extravagant meals for which Jason may or may not be home for, and the rest of his staff waited on him hand and foot, pushing themselves to be noticed by the man who saw everything but handed out praise sparingly because his standards were exacting.

"Don't be ridiculous, Sophie," he scoffed. "I've seen where you live. You have no food and there is barely room for a person to live. That is not surviving!" he claimed.

Her eyes flashed with the news that he had been inside her tiny cottage, investigating the contents enough to know that she didn't even have a carton of milk in the refrigerator at the moment. "It is my choice and you have no right to judge me!"

Jason took several steps towards her, intimidating her despite her intentions not to let him. "You made your choice when you took the vows to be my obedient and faithful wife," he enunciated.

"That makes me sound like I'm a dog," she countered.

He actually smiled and the humor reached his dark, enigmatic eyes. "I can assure you, I definitely don't consider you a dog in any sense."

Sophie hated the feelings his smile created within her. All those silly butterflies kicked into overdrive simply because of his charming smile. "What do you want from me?" she asked, crossing her hands over her chest as if she could shield herself from his charm.

"I want you to get into the car and come back with me, for starters." He didn't pause to see if she would obey; he turned on his heel and moved in the direction of the waiting limousine.

Sophie watched him for about two steps before she gritted out, "No."

That stopped him. Probably because he'd never heard it before. Definitely not from any of his employees and never had Sophie had the courage to say it during their marriage. Jason turned around and raised one dark eyebrow in mild shock as he took in her stubborn stance. "No?" he asked with deadly and terrifying calm.

Sophie didn't like the amusement still in his eyes. She thought a different tactic might be more effective since her current one was only making him angry or amused, she wasn't positive which. Softening her stance, she turned her eyes to pleading, her palms up in the hope that she could make him understand her position. "Jason, our marriage was a farce and you know it. Let's just let it die as it should."

Instantly his lips firmed in anger. "Because I disagree that it is over. And until I agree, I will not grant you a divorce."

Her eyes widened and her whole body recoiled at his statement. "You can't do that!" But she knew he could. He had enough wealth and influence to do just about anything he wanted.

"Don't challenge me on this, Sophie," he said calmly.

List of Elizabeth Lennox Books

The Texas Tycoon's Temptation

The Royal Cordova Trilogy
Escaping a Royal Wedding
The Man's Outrageous Demands
Mistress to the Prince

The Attracelli Family Series
Never Dare a Tycoon
Falling For the Boss
Risky Negotiations
Proposal to Love
Love's Not Terrifying
Romantic Acquisition

The Billionaire's Terms: Prison or Passion
The Sheik's Love Child
The Sheik's Unfinished Business
The Greek Tycoon's Lover
The Sheik's Sensuous Trap
The Greek's Baby Bargain
The Italian's Bedroom Deal
The Billionaire's Gamble
The Tycoon's Seduction Plan
The Sheik's Rebellious Mistress
The Sheik's Missing Bride
Blackmailed by the Billionaire
The Billionaire's Runaway Bride
The Billionaire's Elusive Lover
The Intimate, Intricate Rescue

The Sisterhood Trilogy
The Sheik's Virgin Lover
The Billionaire's Impulsive Lover
The Russian's Tender Lover
The Billionaire's Gentle Rescue

The Tycoon's Toddler Surprise
The Tycoon's Tender Triumph

The Friends Forever Series
The Sheik's Mysterious Mistress
The Duke's Willful Wife
The Tycoon's Marriage Exchange

The Sheik's Secret Twins
The Russian's Furious Fiancée
The Tycoon's Misunderstood Bride

Love By Accident Series
The Sheik's Pregnant Lover
The Sheik's Furious Bride
The Duke's Runaway Princess

The Russian's Pregnant Mistress

The Lovers Exchange Series
The Earl's Outrageous Lover
The Tycoon's Resistant Lover

The Sheik's Reluctant Lover
The Spanish Tycoon's Temptress

The Berutelli Escape
Resisting The Tycoon's Seduction
The Billionaire's Secretive Enchantress

The Big Apple Brotherhood
The Billionaire's Pregnant Lover
The Sheik's Rediscovered Lover

The Tycoon's Defiant Southern Belle

The Sheik's Dangerous Lover (Novella)

The Thorpe Brothers
His Captive Lover
His Unexpected Lover
His Secretive Lover
His Challenging Lover

The Sheik's Defiant Fiancée (Novella)
The Prince's Resistant Lover (Novella)
The Tycoon's Make-Believe Fiancée (Novella)

The Friendship Series
The Billionaire's Masquerade
The Russian's Dangerous Game
The Sheik's Beautiful Intruder

The Love and Danger Series – Romantic Mysteries
Intimate Desires
Intimate Caresses
Intimate Secrets
Intimate Whispers

The Alfieri Saga
The Italian's Passionate Return (Novella)
Her Gentle Capture
His Reluctant Lover
Her Unexpected Admirer
Her Tender Tyrant
Releasing the Billionaire's Passion (Novella)
His Expectant Lover

The Sheik's Intimate Proposition (Novella)

The Hart Sisters Trilogy
The Billionaire's Secret Marriage
The Italian's Twin Surprise (USA Today™ Best Seller!)
The Forbidden Russian Lover (USA Today™ Best Seller!)

The War, Love, and Harmony Series
Fighting with the Infuriating Prince (Novella)
Dancing with the Dangerous Prince (Novella)
The Sheik's Secret Bride
The Sheik's Angry Bride
The Sheik's Blackmailed Bride
The Sheik's Convenient Bride

The Boarding School Series – September 2015 to January 2016
The Boarding School Series Introduction
The Greek's Forgotten Wife
The Duke's Blackmailed Bride
The Russian's Runaway Bride
The Sheik's Baby Surprise
The Tycoon's Captured Heart

Printed in the USA
CPSIA information can be obtained
at www.ICGtesting.com
LVHW010237220724
786147LV00017B/406